How to Eat a Poem

A Smorgasbord of Tasty and Delicious Poems for Young Readers

Edited by
The American Poetry & Literacy Project
and
The Academy of American Poets

with a foreword by
U.S. Poet Laureate Ted Kooser

DOVER PUBLICATIONS, INC.
Mineola, New York

EDITORS OF THIS VOLUME

ANDREW CARROLL,
The American Poetry & Literacy Project

CHARLES FLOWERS, DOUGLAS KORB,
The Academy of American Poets

ACKNOWLEDGMENTS: see page 80

Copyright

Copyright © 2006 by Dover Publications, Inc.

Bibliographical Note

How to Eat a Poem: A Smorgasbord of Tasty and Delicious Poems for Young Readers is a new work, first published by Dover Publications, Inc., in 2006.

Library of Congress Cataloging-in-Publication Data

How to eat a poem : a smorgasbord of tasty and delicious poems for young readers / edited by the American Poetry & Literacy Project and the Academy of American Poets ; with a foreword by Ted Kooser.
    p. cm.
   Includes bibliographical references and index.
   ISBN-13: 978-0-486-45159-6
   ISBN-10: 0-486-45159-3
    1. Young adult poetry, American. 2. Children's poetry, American. I. American Poetry & Literacy Project. II. Academy of American Poets.

PS586.3H69 2006
811'.540809283—dc22

                                                                        2006003940

Manufactured in the United States by Courier Corporation
45159310   2015
www.doverpublications.com

Foreword

A poem, like food, can nourish us. It can be an apple, a hamburger, a salad, or a four-course meal. But it can also be popcorn or a piece of candy. To eat a poem is to read it and swallow it whole, as Eve Merriam's wonderful poem (that gives this anthology its title) illustrates. The more we read poetry, the more we get from each poem, and over time, we develop a life-affirming relationship to poetry.

In my role as Poet Laureate, I've tried to get across a few of my beliefs about poetry:
    It should be fun.
    It should communicate an idea or offer an image.
    It is important to read poetry in order to write it well.

This anthology embodies all of those ideas, and I hope that reading it will bring you plenty of enjoyment. If you don't get some pleasure out of a particular poem after the first (or even second or third!) time you read it, set it aside and try another. Like eating, reading a poem is a personal experience, and nobody says you should have to like it right away.

What I especially like about this collection of poems is its ability to show the world around us in new ways, and also how it captures the relationships between us. Poetry isn't anything and everything, but it can certainly describe just about anything and everything as if we were seeing it for the first time.

So pull up a chair. Dig in. I hope you're hungry.

TED KOOSER
U.S. Poet Laureate

I, too, dislike it.
  Reading it, however, with a perfect contempt for it, one dis-
                                                    covers in
it, after all, a place for the genuine.

–from "Poetry" by Marianne Moore

Contents

MAGIC WORDS
Poems About Poetry, Books, Words, and Imagination

MY HEART LEAPS UP
Poems About the Beauty of the Natural World

I THINK OVER AGAIN
MY SMALL ADVENTURES
Poems About Travel, Adventure, Sports, and Play

HOPE IS THE THING WITH FEATHERS
Poems About Love, Friendship, Sadness, Hope, and Other Emotions

MAGIC WORDS
Poems About Poetry, Books, Words, and Imagination

The First Book

Rita Dove

Open it.

Go ahead, it won't bite.
Well . . . maybe a little.

More a nip, like. A tingle.
It's pleasurable, really.

You see, it keeps on opening.
You may fall in.

Sure, it's hard to get started;
remember learning to use

knife and fork? Dig in:
You'll never reach bottom.

It's not like it's the end of the world—
just the world as you think

you know it.

There Is No Frigate Like a Book

Emily Dickinson

There is no frigate like a book
  To take us lands away,
Nor any coursers like a page
  Of prancing poetry.
This traverse may the poorest take
  Without oppress of toll;
How frugal is the chariot
  That bears a human soul!

from **"Magic Words"**

Inuit (Eskimo) passage, translated by Edward Field

In the very earliest time,
When both people and animals lived on earth,
A person could become an animal if he wanted to
And an animal could become a human being.
Sometimes they were people
And sometimes animals
And there was no difference.
All spoke the same language.
That was the time when words were like magic.
The human mind had mysterious powers.
A word spoken by chance
Might have strange consequences.
It would suddenly come alive
And what people wanted to happen could happen
All you had to do was say it.

Introduction to Poetry

Billy Collins

I ask them to take a poem
and hold it up to the light
like a color slide
or press an ear against its hive.

I say drop a mouse into a poem
and watch him probe his way out,

or walk inside the poem's room
and feel the walls for a light switch.

I want them to waterski
across the surface of a poem
waving at the author's name on the shore.

But all they want to do
is tie the poem to a chair with rope
and torture a confession out of it.

They begin beating it with a hose
to find out what it really means.

The Poem

Amy Lowell

It is only a little twig
With a green bud at the end;
But if you plant it,
And water it,
And set it where the sun will be above it,
It will grow into a tall bush
With many flowers,
And leaves which thrust hither and thither
Sparkling.
From its roots will come freshness,
And beneath it the grass-blades
Will bend and recover themselves,
And clash one upon another
In the blowing wind.

But if you take my twig
And throw it into a closet
With mousetraps and blunted tools,
It will shrivel and waste
And, some day,
When you open the door,
You will think it an old twisted nail,
And sweep it into the dust bin
With other rubbish.

Ars Poetica

Archibald MacLeish

A poem should be palpable and mute
As a globed fruit

Dumb
As old medallions to the thumb

Silent as the sleeve-worn stone
Of casement ledges where the moss has grown—

A poem should be wordless
As the flight of birds

A poem should be motionless in time
As the moon climbs

Leaving, as the moon releases
Twig by twig the night-entangled trees,

Leaving, as the moon behind the winter leaves,
Memory by memory the mind—

A poem should be motionless in time
As the moon climbs

A poem should be equal to:
Not true

For all the history of grief
An empty doorway and a maple leaf

For love
The leaning grasses and two lights above the sea

A poem should not mean
But be

How to Eat a Poem

Eve Merriam

Don't be polite.
Bite in.
Pick it up with your fingers and lick the juice that
     may run down your chin.
It is ready and ripe now, whenever you are.

You do not need a knife or fork or spoon
or plate or napkin or tablecloth.

For there is no core
or stem
or rind
or pit
or seed
or skin
to throw away.

Six Words

Lloyd Schwartz

yes
no
maybe
sometimes
always
never

Never?
Yes.
Always?
No.
Sometimes?
Maybe—

maybe
never
sometimes.
Yes—
no
always:

always
maybe.
No—
never
yes.
Sometimes,

8

sometimes
(always)
yes.
Maybe
never . . .
No,

no—
sometimes.
Never.
Always?
Maybe.
Yes—

yes no
maybe sometimes
always never.

Prickled Pickles Don't Smile

Nikki Giovanni

Never tickle,
a prickled pickle
'cause prickled pickles
Don't smile

Never goad
a loaded toad
when he has to walk
A whole mile

Froggies go courting
with weather reporting
that indicates
There are no snows

But always remember
the month of December
is very hard
On your nose

Thirteen Ways of Looking at a Blackbird

Wallace Stevens

1

Among twenty snowy mountains,
The only moving thing
Was the eye of the blackbird.

2

I was of three minds,
Like a tree
In which there are three blackbirds.

3

The blackbird whirled in the autumn winds.
It was a small part of the pantomime.

4

A man and a woman
Are one.
A man and a woman and a blackbird
Are one.

5

I do not know which to prefer,
The beauty of inflections
Or the beauty of innuendoes,
The blackbird whistling
Or just after.

6

Icicles filled the long window
With barbaric glass.
The shadow of the blackbird
Crossed it, to and fro.
The mood
Traced in the shadow
An indecipherable cause.

7

O thin men of Haddam,
Why do you imagine golden birds?
Do you not see how the blackbird
Walks around the feet
Of the women about you?

8

I know noble accents
And lucid, inescapable rhythms;
But I know, too,
That the blackbird is involved
In what I know.

9

When the blackbird flew out of sight,
It marked the edge
Of one of many circles.

10

At the sight of blackbirds
Flying in a green light,
Even the bawds of euphony
Would cry out sharply.

11

He rode over Connecticut
In a glass coach.
Once, a fear pierced him
In that he mistook
The shadow of his equipage
For blackbirds.

12

The river is moving.
The blackbird must be flying.

13

It was evening all afternoon.
It was snowing
And it was going to snow.
The blackbird sat
In the cedar-limbs.

This Is Just to Say

William Carlos Williams

I have eaten
the plums
that were in
the icebox

and which
you were probably
saving
for breakfast

Forgive me
they were delicious
so sweet
and so cold

Variations on a Theme
by William Carlos Williams

Kenneth Koch

1

I chopped down the house that you had been saving to live
    in next summer.
I am sorry, but it was morning, and I had nothing to do
and its wooden beams were so inviting.

2

We laughed at the hollyhocks together
and then I sprayed them with lye.
Forgive me. I simply do not know what I am doing.

3

I gave away the money that you had been saving to live on
    for the next ten years.
The man who asked for it was shabby
and the firm March wind on the porch was so juicy and cold.

4

Last evening we went dancing and I broke your leg.
Forgive me. I was clumsy, and
I wanted you here in the wards, where I am the doctor!

Today is Very Boring

Jack Prelutsky

Today is very boring,
it's a very boring day,
there is nothing much to look at,
there is nothing much to say,
there's a peacock on my sneakers,
there's a penguin on my head,
there's a dormouse on my doorstep,
I am going back to bed.

Today is very boring,
it is boring through and through,
there is absolutely nothing
that I think I want to do,
I see giants riding rhinos,
and an ogre with a sword,
there's a dragon blowing smoke rings,
I am positively bored.

Today is very boring,
I can hardly help but yawn,
there's a flying saucer landing
in the middle of my lawn,
a volcano just erupted
less than half a mile away,
and I think I felt an earthquake,
it's a very boring day.

The Unwritten

W. S. Merwin

Inside this pencil
crouch words that have never been written
never been spoken
never been taught

they're hiding

they're awake in there
dark in the dark
hearing us
but they won't come out
not for love not for time not for fire

even when the dark has worn away
they'll still be there
hiding in the air
multitudes in days to come may walk through them
breathe them
be none the wiser

what script can it be
that they won't unroll
in what language
would I recognize it
would I be able to follow it
to make out the real names
of everything

maybe there aren't
many
it could be that there's only one word
and it's all we need
it's here in this pencil

every pencil in the world
is like this

Write, Do Write

Marilyn Chin

And to you, the exiled one in Singkiang, waiting twenty years
    for the sun,
a large, hideous lantern strutting
over the barbarian wilderness—

wherever you are, don't forget me, please—
on heaven's stationery, with earth's chalk,
write, do write.

My Heart Leaps Up When I Behold

William Wordsworth

My heart leaps up when I behold
    A rainbow in the sky;
So was it when my life began;
So it is now I am a man;
So be it when. I shall grow old,
    Or let me die!
The Child is father of the Man;
And I could wish my days to be
Bound each to each by natural piety.

W. D., Don't Fear That Animal

W. D. Snodgrass

My hat leaps up when I behold
    A rhino in the sky;
When crocodiles upon the wing
Perch on my windowsill to sing,
All my loose ends turn blue and cold;
    I don't know why.

My knuckles whiten should I hark
    Some lonely python's cry;
Should a migrating wedge of moose
Honk, it can shake my molars loose—
Or when, at Heaven's gate, the shark
    Doth pine and sigh.

My socks may slide off at the sight
    Of giant squids on high
Or baby scorpions bubbling up
Inside my morning coffee cup—
Somehow, it spoils my appetite;
    My throat gets dry.

At dawn. I lift my gaze in air
    Cock Robin to espy
And mark instead some bright-eyed grizzly;
The hairs back of my neck turn bristly.
That's foolish since we know that they're
    More scared than I.

Such innocent creatures mean no harm;
    They wouldn't hurt a fly.
Still, when I find myself between a
Playful assembly of hyena,
I can't help feeling some alarm;
    I've got to try.

Swift Things Are Beautiful

Elizabeth Coatsworth

Swift things are beautiful:
Swallows and deer,
And lightning that falls
Bright-veined and clear,
Rivers and meteors,
Wind in the wheat,
The strong-withered horse,
The runner's sure feet.

And slow things are beautiful:
The closing of day,
The pause of the wave
That curves downward to spray,
The ember that crumbles,
The opening flower,
And the ox that moves on
In the quiet of power.

Four Seasons of Haiku

Summer
Kawabata Bōsha

Fireflies at nightfall—
a chair of bright beads
along the water's edge.

Autumn
Arakida Moritake

A colorful falling leaf
drifts to a branch—
No, a butterfly!

Winter
Takarai Kikaku

The cold moon shines
on the matting on the floor,
thin shadows of the pines.

Spring
Matsuo Bashō

The temple bell stops;
but the ringing echoes
from out of the blossoms.

Nothing Gold Can Stay

Robert Frost

Nature's first green is gold,
Her hardest hue to hold.
Her early leaf's a flower;
But only so an hour.
Then leaf subsides to leaf.
So Eden sank to grief,
So dawn goes down to day.
Nothing gold can stay.

The Desert Is My Mother

Pat Mora

I say feed me.
She serves red prickly pear on a spiked cactus.

I say tease me.
She sprinkles raindrops in my face on a sunny day.

I say frighten me.
She shouts thunder, flashes lightning.

I say hold me.
She whispers, "Lie in my arms."

I say heal me.
She gives me chamomile, oregano, peppermint.

I say caress me.
She strokes my skin with her warm breath.

I say make me beautiful.
She offers turquoise for my fingers,
    a pink blossom for my hair.

I say sing to me.
She chants her windy songs.

I say teach me.
She blooms in the sun's glare,
    the snow's silence,
    the driest sand.

The desert is my mother.
El desierto es mi madre.
The desert is my strong mother.

El desierto es mi madre

Pat Mora

Le digo, dame de comer.
Me sirve rojas tunas en nopal espinoso.

Le digo, juguetea conmigo.
Me salpica la cara con gotitas de lluvia en día asoleado.

Le digo, asústame.
Me grita con truenos y me tira relámpagos.

Le digo, abrázame.
Me susurra, "Acuéstate aquí."

Le digo, cúrame.
Me da manzanilla, orégano, yerbabuena.

Le digo, acaríciame.
Me roza la cara con su cálido aliento.

Le digo, hazme bella.
Me ofrece turquesa para mis dedos,
    una flor rosada para mi cabello.

Le digo, cántame.
Me arrulla con sus canciones de viento.

Le digo, enséñame.
Y florece en el brillo del sol,
    en el silencio de la nieve,
    en las arenas más secas.

El desierto es mi madre.

El desierto es mi madre poderosa.

maggie and milly and molly and may

E. E. Cummings

maggie and milly and molly and may
went down to the beach(to play one day)

and maggie discovered a shell that sang
so sweetly she couldn't remember her troubles,and

milly befriended a stranded star
whose rays five languid fingers were;

and molly was chased by a horrible thing
which raced sideways while blowing bubbles:and

may came home with a smooth round stone
as small as a world and as large as alone.

For whatever we lose(like a you or a me)
it's always ourselves we find in the sea.

A Jelly-Fish

Marianne Moore

Visible, invisible,
    a fluctuating charm
an amber-tinctured amethyst
    inhabits it, your arm
approaches and it opens
    and it closes; you had meant
to catch it and it quivers;
    you abandon your intent.

The Eagle

Alfred, Lord Tennyson

He clasps the crag with crooked hands;
Close to the sun in lonely hands,
Ringed with the azure world, he stands.

The wrinkled sea beneath him crawls;
He watches from his mountain walls,
And like a thunderbolt he falls.

Eagle Poem

Joy Harjo

To pray you open your whole self
To sky, to earth, to sun, to moon
To one whole voice that is you.
And know there is more
That you can't see, can't hear,
Can't know except in moments
Steadily growing, and in languages
That aren't always sound but other
Circles of motion.
Like eagle that Sunday morning
Over Salt River. Circled in blue sky
In wind, swept our hearts clean
With sacred wings.
We see you, see ourselves and know
That we must take the utmost care
And kindness in all things.
Breathe in, knowing we are made of
All this, and breathe, knowing
We are truly blessed because we
Were born, and die soon within a
True circle of motion,
Like eagle rounding out the morning
Inside us.
We pray that it will be done
In beauty.
In beauty.

Considering the Snail

Thom Gunn

The snail pushes through a green
night, for the grass is heavy
with water and meets over
the bright path he makes, where rain
has darkened the earth's dark. He
moves in a wood of desire,

pale antlers barely stirring
as he hums. I cannot tell
what power is at work, drenched there
with purpose, knowing nothing.
What is a snail's fury? All
I think is that if later

I parted the blades above
the tunnel and saw the thin
trail of broken white across
litter, I would never have
imagined the slow passion
to that deliberate progress.

The Porcupine

Ogden Nash

Any hound a porcupine nudges
Can't be blamed for harboring grudges.
I know one hound that laughed all winter
At a porcupine that sat on a splinter.

The Crocodile

Lewis Carroll

How doth the little crocodile
    Improve his shining tail,
And pour the waters of the Nile
    On every golden scale!

How cheerfully he seems to grin,
    How neatly spreads his claws,
And welcomes little fishes in,
    With gently smiling jaws!

The Tyger

William Blake

Tyger! Tyger! burning bright
In the forests of the night,
What immortal hand or eye
Could frame thy fearful symmetry?

In what distant deeps or skies
Burnt the fire of thine eyes?
On what wings dare he aspire?
What the hand dare seize the fire?

And what shoulder, and what art,
Could twist the sinews of thy heart?
And, when thy heart began to beat,
What dread hand? and what dread feet?

What the hammer? what the chain?
In what furnace was thy brain?
What the anvil? what dread grasp
Dare its deadly terrors clasp?

When the stars threw down their spears,
And watered heaven with their tears,
Did he smile his work to see?
Did he who made the lamb make thee?

Tyger! Tyger! burning bright
In the forests of the night,
What immortal hand or eye,
Dare frame thy fearful symmetry?

Steam Shovel

Charles Malam

The dinosaurs are not all dead.
I saw one raise its iron head
To watch me walking down the road
Beyond our house today.
Its jaws were dripping with a load
Of earth and grass that it had cropped.
It must have heard me where I stopped,
Snorted white steam my way,
And stretched its long neck out to see,
And chewed, and grinned quite amiably.

Cartoon Physics, part 1

Nick Flynn

Children under, say, *ten,* shouldn't know
that the universe is ever-expanding,
inexorably pushing into the vacuum, galaxies

swallowed by galaxies, whole

solar systems collapsing, all of it
acted out in silence. At ten we are still learning

the rules of cartoon animation,

that if a man draws a door on a rock
only he can pass through it.
Anyone else who tries

will crash into the rock. Ten-year-olds
should stick with burning houses, car wrecks,
ships going down—earthbound, tangible

disasters, arenas

where they can be heroes. You can run
back into a burning house, sinking ships

have lifeboats, the trucks will come
with their ladders, if you jump

you will be saved. A child

places her hand on the roof of a schoolbus,
& drives across a city of sand. She knows

the exact spot it will skid, at which point
the bridge will give, who will swim to safety
& who will be pulled under by sharks. She will learn

that if a man runs off the edge of a cliff
he will not fall

until he notices his mistake.

The Falling Star

Sara Teasdale

I saw a star slide down the sky,
Blinding the north as it went by,
Too burning and too quick to hold,
Too lovely to be bought or sold,
Good only to make wishes on
And then forever to be gone.

Halley's Comet

Stanley Kunitz

Miss Murphy in first grade
wrote its name in chalk
across the board and told us
it was roaring down the stormtracks
of the Milky Way at frightful speed
and if it wandered off its course
and smashed into the earth
there'd be no school tomorrow.
A red-bearded preacher from the hills
with a wild look in his eyes
stood in the public square
at the playground's edge
proclaiming he was sent by God
to save every one of us,
even the little children.
"Repent, ye sinners!" he shouted,
waving his hand-lettered sign.
At supper I felt sad to think
that it was probably
the last meal I'd share
with my mother and my sisters;
but I felt excited too
and scarcely touched my plate.
So mother scolded me
and sent me early to my room.
The whole family's asleep
except for me. They never heard me steal

into the stairwell hall and climb
the ladder to the fresh night air.
Look for me, Father, on the roof
of the red brick building
at the foot of Green Street—
that's where we live, you know, on the top floor.
I'm the boy in the white flannel gown
sprawled on this coarse gravel bed
searching the night sky,
waiting for the world to end.

When I Heard the Learn'd Astronomer

Walt Whitman

When I heard the learn'd astronomer,
When the proofs, the figures, were ranged in columns before
    me,
When I was shown the charts and diagrams, to add, divide,
    and measure them,
When I sitting heard the astronomer where he lectured with
    much applause in the lecture-room,
How soon unaccountable I became tired and sick,
Till rising and gliding out I wander'd off by myself,
In the mystical moist night-air, and from time to time,
Look'd up in perfect silence at the stars.

I THINK OVER AGAIN
MY SMALL ADVENTURES
Poems About Travel, Adventure, Sports, and Play

Sick

Shel Silverstein

"I cannot go to school today,"
Said little Peggy Ann McKay.
"I have the measles and the mumps,
A gash, a rash and purple bumps.
My mouth is wet, my throat is dry,
I'm going blind in my right eye.
My tonsils are as big as rocks,
I've counted sixteen chicken pox
And there's one more—that's seventeen,
And don't you think my face looks green?
My leg is cut, my eyes are blue—
It might be instamatic flu.
I cough and sneeze and gasp and choke,
I'm sure that my left leg is broke—
My hip hurts when I move my chin,
My belly button's caving in,
My back is wrenched, my ankle's sprained,
My 'pendix pains each time it rains.
My nose is cold, my toes are numb,
I have a sliver in my thumb.
My neck is stiff, my voice is weak,
I hardly whisper when I speak.

My tongue is filling up my mouth,
I think my hair is falling out.
My elbow's bent. My spine ain't straight.
My temperature is one-o-eight.
My brain is shrunk, I cannot hear,
There is a hole inside my ear.
I have a hangnail, and my heart is—what?
What's that? What's that you say?
You say today is . . . Saturday?
G'bye, I'm going out to play!"

Travel

Edna St. Vincent Millay

The railroad track is miles away,
    And the day is loud with voices speaking,
Yet there isn't a train goes by all day
    But I hear its whistle shrieking.

All night there isn't a train goes by,
    Though the night is still for sleep and dreaming,
But I see its cinders red on the sky,
    And hear its engine steaming,

My heart is warm with the friends I make,
    And better friends I'll not be knowing,
Yet there isn't a train I wouldn't take,
    No matter where it's going.

Insomnia

Marilyn Nelson

My mind points
in countless directions,
while I toss on the gray hard water
of sleep.
I want to go traveling
down the highway
in my leg,
tumbleweed and sagebrush
and the last chance fillup station,
a smiling stranger
in a ten gallon hat
waving
as I go past,
farther and farther,
miles and miles,
toward the point
where all the lines
converge.

Harlem Night Song

Langston Hughes

Come, Let us roam the night together
Singing.

I love you.

Across
The Harlem roof-tops
Moon is shining.
Night sky is blue.
Stars are great drops
Of golden dew.

Down the street
A band is playing

I love you.

Come,
Let us roam the night together
Singing.

The Rider

Naomi Shihab Nye

A boy told me
if he roller-skated fast enough
his loneliness couldn't catch up to him,

the best reason I ever heard
for trying to be a champion.

What I wonder tonight
pedaling hard down King William Street
is if it translates to bicycles.

A victory! To leave your loneliness
panting behind you on some street corner
while you float free into a cloud of sudden azaleas,
pink petals that have never felt loneliness,
no matter how slowly they fell.

The Jogger on Riverside Drive, 5:00 A.M.

Agha Shahid Ali

The dark scissors of his legs
cut the moon's

raw silk, highways of wind
torn into lanes, his feet

pushing down the shadow
whose patterns he becomes

while trucks, one by one,
pass him by,

headlights pouring
from his face, his eyes

cracked as the Hudson
wraps street lamps

in its rippled blue shells,
the summer's thin, thin veins

bursting with dawn,
he, now suddenly free,

from the air, from himself,
his heart beating far, far

behind him.

First Love

Carl Lindner

Before sixteen
I was fast
enough to fake
my shadow out
and I could read
every crack and ripple
in that catch of asphalt.
I owned
the slanted rim
knew
the dead spot in the backboard.
Always the ball
came back.

Every day I loved
to sharpen
my shooting eye,
waiting
for the touch.
Set shot, jump shot,
layup, hook—
after a while
I could feel
the ball hunger-
ing to clear
the lip of the rim,
the two of us
falling through.

Skier

Robert Francis

He swings down like the flourish of a pen
Signing a signature in white on white.

The silence of his skis reciprocates
The silence of the world around him.

Wind is his one competitor
In the cool winding and unwinding down.

On incandescent feet he falls
Unfalling, trailing white foam, white fire.

Skater

Ted Kooser

She was all in black but for a yellow ponytail
that trailed from her cap, and bright blue gloves
that she held out wide, the feathery fingers spread,
as surely she stepped, click-clack, onto the frozen
top of the world. And there, with a clatter of blades,
she began to braid a loose path that broadened
into a meadow of curls. Across the ice she swooped
and then turned back and, halfway, bent her legs
and leapt into the air the way a crane leaps, blue gloves
lifting her lightly, and turned a snappy half-turn
there in the wind before coming down, arms wide,
skating backward right out of that moment, smiling back
at the woman she'd been just an instant before.

The Acrobat

Wislawa Szymborska

From trapeze to
to trapeze, in the hush that
that follows the drum roll's sudden pause, through
through the startled air, more swiftly than
than his body's weight, which once again
again is late for its own fall.

Solo. Or even less than solo,
less, because he's crippled, missing
missing wings, missing them so much
that he can't miss the chance
to soar on shamefully unfeathered
naked vigilance alone.

Arduous ease,
watchful agility,
and calculated inspiration. Do you see
how he waits to pounce in flight; do you know
how he plots from head to toe
against his very being; do you know, do you see
how cunningly he weaves himself through his own former
    shape
and works to seize this swaying world
by stretching out the arms he has conceived—

beautiful beyond belief at this passing
at this very passing moment that's just passed.

Baseball

Linda Pastan

When you tried to tell me
baseball was a metaphor

for life: the long, dusty travail
around the bases, for instance,

to try to go home again;
the Sacrifice for which you win

approval but not applause;
the way the light closes down

in the last days of the season—
I didn't believe you.

It's just a way of passing
the time, I said.

And you said: that's it.
Yes.

Casey at the Bat

Ernest Lawrence Thayer

The outlook wasn't brilliant for the Mudville nine that day;
The score stood four to two with but one inning more to play.
And then when Cooney died at first, and Barrows did the
  same,
A sickly silence fell upon the patrons of the game.

A straggling few got up to go in deep despair. The rest
Clung to the hope which springs eternal in the human breast;
They thought if only Casey could but get a whack at that—
We'd put up even money now with Casey at the bat.

But Flynn preceded Casey, as did also Jimmy Blake,
And the former was a lulu and the latter was a cake;
So upon that stricken multitude grim melancholy sat,
For there seemed but little chance of Casey's getting to the
  bat.

But Flynn let drive a single, to the wonderment of all,
And Blake, the much despis-ed, tore the cover off the ball;
And when the dust had lifted, and the men saw what had
  occurred,
There was Johnnie safe at second and Flynn a-hugging third.

Then from 5,000 throats and more there rose a lusty yell;
It rumbled through the valley, it rattled in the dell;
It knocked upon the mountain and recoiled upon the flat,
For Casey, mighty Casey, was advancing to the bat.

There was ease in Casey's manner as he stepped into his
    place;
There was pride in Casey's bearing and a smile on Casey's
    face.
And when, responding to the cheers, he lightly doffed his hat,
No stranger in the crowd could doubt 'twas Casey at the bat.

Ten thousand eyes were on him as he rubbed his hands with
    dirt;
Five thousand tongues applauded when he wiped them on
    his shirt.
Then while the writhing pitcher ground the ball into his hip,
Defiance gleamed in Casey's eye, a sneer curled Casey's lip.

And now the leather-covered sphere came hurtling through
    the air,
And Casey stood a-watching it in haughty grandeur there.
Close by the sturdy batsman the ball unheeded sped—
"That ain't my style," said Casey. "Strike one," the umpire
    said.

From the benches, black with people, there went up a muf-
    fled roar,
Like the beating of the storm-waves on a stern and distant
    shore.
"Kill him! Kill the umpire!" shouted someone on the stand;
And it's likely they'd have killed him had not Casey raised
    his hand.

With a smile of Christian charity great Casey's visage shown;
He stilled the rising tumult; he bade the game go on;
He signaled to the pitcher, and once more the spheroid flew;
But Casey still ignored it, and the umpire said, "Strike two."

"Fraud!" cried the maddened thousands, and echo answered
    fraud;
But one scornful look from Casey and the audience was
    awed.
They saw his face grow stern and cold, they saw his muscles
    strain,
And they knew that Casey wouldn't let that ball go by again.

The sneer is gone from Casey's lip, his teeth are clenched in
    hate;
He pounds with cruel violence his bat upon the plate.
And now the pitcher holds the ball, and now he lets it go,
And now the air is shattered by the force of Casey's blow.

Oh, somewhere in this favored land the sun is shining bright;
The band is playing somewhere, and somewhere hearts are
    light,
And somewhere men are laughing, and somewhere children
    shout;
But there is no joy in Mudville—mighty Casey has struck out.

One Art

Elizabeth Bishop

The art of losing isn't hard to master;
so many things seem filled with the intent
to be lost that their loss is no disaster.

Lose something every day. Accept the fluster
of lost door keys, the hour badly spent.
The art of losing isn't hard to master.

Then practice losing farther, losing faster:
places, and names, and where it was you meant
to travel. None of these will bring disaster.

I lost my mother's watch. And look! my last,
or next-to-last, of three loved houses went.
The art of losing isn't hard to master.

I lost two cities, lovely ones. And, vaster,
some realms I owned, two rivers, a continent.
I miss them, but it wasn't a disaster.

—Even losing you (the joking voice, a gesture
I love) I shan't have lied. It's evident
the art of losing's not too hard to master
though it may look like (*Write* it!) like disaster.

I Think Over Again My Small Adventures

Anonymous. (North American Indian; 19th century)

I think over again my small adventures,
My fears,
Those small ones that seemed so big,
For all the vital things
I had to get and to reach;
And yet there is only one great thing,
The only thing,
To live to see the great day that dawns
And the light that fills the world.

Bed In Summer

Robert Louis Stevenson

In winter I get up at night
And dress by yellow candle-light.
In summer, quite the other way,
I have to go to bed by day.

I have to go to bed and see
The birds still hopping on the tree,
Or hear the grown-up people's feet
Still going past me in the street.

And does it not seem hard to you,
When all the sky is clear and blue,
And I should like so much to play,
To have to go to bed by day?

from **The Bed Book**

Sylvia Plath

Most Beds are Beds
For sleeping or resting,
But the *best* Beds are much
More interesting!

Not just a white little
Tucked-in-tight little
Nighty-night little
Turn-out-the-light little
    Bed—

    Instead
A Bed for Fishing
A Bed for Cats,
A Bed for a Troupe of
    Acrobats.

The *right* sort of Bed
(If you see what I mean)
Is a Bed that might
Be a Submarine

Nosing through water
Clear and green,
Silver and glittery
As a sardine.

Or a Jet-Propelled Bed
For Visiting Mars
With mosquito nest
For the shooting stars. . . .

Summons

Robert Francis

Keep me from going to sleep too soon
Or if I go to sleep too soon
Come wake me up. Come any hour
Of night. Come whistling up the road.
Stomp on the porch. Bang on the door.
Make me get out of bed and come
And let you in and light a light.
Tell me the northern lights are on
And make me look. Or tell me clouds
Are doing something to the moon
They never did before, and show me.
See that I see. Talk to me till
I'm half as wide awake as you
And start to dress wondering why
I ever went to bed at all.
Tell me the walking is superb.
Not only tell me but persuade me.
You know I'm not too hard persuaded.

HOPE IS THE THING WITH FEATHERS
Poems About Love, Friendship, Sadness, Hope, and Other Emotions

Shirley Said

Dennis Doyle

Who wrote "kick me" on my back?
Who put a spider in my mac?
Who's the one who pulls my hair?
Tries to trip me everywhere?
Who runs up to me and strikes me?
That boy there—I think he likes me.

Oranges

Gary Soto

The first time I walked
With a girl, I was twelve,
Cold, and weighted down
With two oranges in my jacket.
December. Frost cracking
Beneath my steps, my breath
Before me, then gone,
As I walked toward
Her house, the one whose
Porch light burned yellow
Night and day, in any weather.
A dog barked at me, until
She came out pulling
At her gloves, face bright
With rouge. I smiled,
Touched her shoulder, and led
Her down the street, across
A used car lot and a line
Of newly planted trees,
Until we were breathing
Before a drugstore. We
Entered, the tiny bell
Bringing a saleslady
Down a narrow aisle of goods.
I turned to the candies
Tiered like bleachers,
And asked what she wanted—
Light in her eyes, a smile
Starting at the corners

Of her mouth. I fingered
A nickel in my pocket,
And when she lifted a chocolate
That cost a dime,
I didn't say anything.
I took the nickel from
My pocket, then an orange,
And set them quietly on
The counter. When I looked up,
The lady's eyes met mine,
And held them, knowing
Very well what it was all
About.
     Outside,
A few cars hissing past,
Fog hanging like old
Coats between the trees.
I took my girl's hand
In mine for two blocks,
Then released it to let
Her unwrap the chocolate.
I peeled my orange
That was so bright against
The gray of December
That, from some distance,
Someone might have thought
I was making a fire in my hands.

The Floor and the Ceiling

William Jay Smith

Winter and summer, whatever the weather,
The Floor and the Ceiling were happy together
In a quaint little house on the outskirts of town
With the Floor looking up and the Ceiling looking down.

The Floor bought the Ceiling an ostrich-plumed hat,
And they dined upon drippings of bacon fat,
Diced artichoke hearts and cottage cheese
And hundreds of other such delicacies.

On a screened-in porch in early spring
They would sit at the player piano and sing.
When the Floor cried in French, "Ah, je vous adore!"
The Ceiling replied, "You adorable Floor!"

The years went by as the years they will,
And each little thing was fine until
One evening, enjoying their bacon fat,
The Floor and the Ceiling had a terrible spat.

The Ceiling, loftily looking down,
Said, "You are the lowest Floor in this town!"
The Floor, looking up with a frightening grin,
Said, "Keep up your chatter, and you will cave in!"

So they went off to bed: while the Floor settled down,
The Ceiling packed up her gay wallflower gown;
And tiptoeing out past the Chippendale chair
And the gateleg table, down the stair,

Took a coat from the hook and a hat from the rack,
And flew out the door—farewell to the Floor!—
And flew out the door, and was seen no more,
And flew out the door, and *never* came back!

In a quaint little house on the outskirts of town,
Now the shutters go bang, and the walls tumble down;
And the roses in summer run wild through the room,
But blooming for no one—then why should they bloom?

For what is a Floor now that brambles have grown
Over window and woodwork and chimney of stone?
For what is a Floor when the Floor stands alone?
And what is a Ceiling when the Ceiling has flown?

Annabel Lee

Edgar Allan Poe

It was many and many a year ago,
 In a kingdom by the sea,
That a maiden there lived whom you may know
 By the name of ANNABEL LEE;
And this maiden she lived with no other thought
 Than to love and be loved by me.

I was a child and *she* was a child,
 In this kingdom by the sea:
But we loved with a love that was more than love—
 I and my ANNABEL LEE—
With a love that the wingèd seraphs of Heaven
 Coveted her and me.

And this was the reason that, long ago,
 In this kingdom by the sea,
A wind blew out of a cloud, chilling
 My beautiful ANNABEL LEE;
So that her high-born kinsmen came
 And bore her away from me,
To shut her up in a sepulchre
 In this kingdom by the sea.

The angels, not half so happy in heaven,
 Went envying her and me—
Yes!—that was the reason (as all men know,
 In this kingdom by the sea)
That the wind came out of the cloud by night,
 Chilling and killing my ANNABEL LEE.

But our love it was stronger by far than the love
    Of those who were older than we—
    Of many far wiser than we—
And neither the angels in heaven above.
    Nor the demons down under the sea,
Can ever dissever my soul from the soul
    Of the beautiful ANNABEL LEE:

For the moon never beams, without bringing me dreams
    Of the beautiful ANNABEL LEE;
And the stars never rise, but I feel the bright eyes
    Of the beautiful ANNABEL LEE;
And so, all the night-tide, I lie down by the side
Of my darling—my darling—my life and my bride,
    In her sepulchre there by the sea,
    In her tomb by the sounding sea.

Sympathy

Paul Laurence Dunbar

I know what the caged bird feels, alas!
When the sun is bright on the upland slopes;
When the wind stirs soft through the springing grass
And the river flows like a stream of glass;
When the first bird sings and the first bud opes,
And the faint perfume from its chalice steals—
I know what the caged bird feels!

I know why the caged bird beats his wing
Till its blood is red on the cruel bars;
For he must fly back to his perch and cling
When he fain would be on the bough a-swing;
And a pain still throbs in the old, old scars
And they pulse again with a keener sting—
I know why he beats his wing!

I know why the caged bird sings, ah me,
When his wing is bruised and his bosom sore,—
When he beats his bars and would be free;
It is not a carol of joy or glee,
But a prayer that he sends from his deep heart's core,
But a plea, that upward to Heaven he flings—
I know why the caged bird sings!

Ozymandias

Percy Bysshe Shelley

I met a traveler from an antique land
Who said: Two vast and trunkless legs of stone
Stand in the desert. Near them, on the sand,
Half sunk, a shattered visage lies, whose frown,
And wrinkled lip, and sneer of cold command,
Tell that its sculptor well those passions read
Which yet survive, stamped on these lifeless things,
The hand that mocked them and the heart that fed;
And on the pedestal these words appear:
"My name is Ozymandias, king of kings:
Look on my works, ye Mighty, and despair!"
Nothing beside remains. Round the decay
Of that colossal wreck, boundless and bare
The lone and level sands stretch far away.

Spring and Fall

Gerard Manley Hopkins

To a Young Child

Márgaret, áre you gríeving
Over Goldengrove unleaving?
Leáves, líke the things of man, you
With your fresh thoughts care for, can you?
Áh! ás the heart grows older
It will come to such sights colder
By and by, nor spare a sigh
Though worlds of wanwood leafmeal lie;
And yet you *will* weep and know why.
Now no matter, child, the name:
Sórrow's spríngs áre the same.
Nor mouth had, no nor mind, expressed
What heart heard of, ghost guessed:
It ís the blight man was born for,
It is Margaret you mourn for.

Trees

Walter Dean Myers

I am a tree
Strong limbed and deeply rooted
My fruit is bittersweet
I am your mother

You are a tree
A sapling by the river
With buds straining for the winter sun
You are my child
Together we are a forest
Against the wind

With Kit, Age Seven, At the Beach

William Stafford

We would climb the highest dune,
from there to gaze and come down:
the ocean was performing;
we contributed our climb.

Waves leapfrogged and came
straight out of the storm.
What should our gaze mean?
Kit waited for me to decide.

Standing on such a hill,
what would you tell your child?
That was an absolute vista.
Those waves raced far, and cold.

"How far could you swim, Daddy,
in such a storm?"

"As far as was needed," I said,
and as I talked, I swam.

At the End of the Weekend

Ted Kooser

It is Sunday afternoon,
and I suddenly miss
my distant son, who at ten
has just this instant buzzed
my house in a flying
cardboard box, dipping
one wing to look down over
my shimmering roof, the yard,
the car in the drive. In his room
three hundred miles from me,
he tightens his helmet,
grips the controls, turns
loops and rolls. My windows
rattle. On days like this,
the least quick shadow crossing
the page makes me look up
at the sky like a goose,
squinting to see that flash
that I dream is his thought of me
daring to fall through the distance,
then climbing, full throttle, away.

Little Old Letter

Langston Hughes

It was yesterday morning
I looked in my box for mail.
The letter that I found there
Made me turn right pale.

Just a little old letter,
Wasn't even one page long—
But it made me wish
I was in my grave: and gone.

I turned it over,
Not a word writ on the back.
I never felt so lonesome
Since I was born black.

Just a pencil and paper,
You don't need no gun nor knife—
A little old letter
Can take a person's life.

from "I Am a Black Woman"

Mari Evans

I
am a black woman
tall as a cypress
strong
beyond all definition still
defying place
and time
and circumstance
    assailed
        impervious
            indestructible
Look
    on me and be
renewed

homage to my hips

Lucille Clifton

these hips are big hips.
they need space to
move around in.
they don't fit into little
petty places. these hips
are free hips.
they don't like to be held back.
these hips have never been enslaved,
they go where they want to go
they do what they want to do.
these hips are mighty hips.
these hips are magic hips.
i have known them
to put a spell on a man and
spin him like a top!

Childhood Morning—Homebush

James McAuley

The half-moon is a muted lamp
Motionless behind a veil.
As the eastern sky grows pale,
I hear the slow train's puffing stamp

Gathering speed. A bulbul sings,
Raiding persimmon and fig.
The rooster in full glossy rig
Crows triumph at the state of things.

I make no comment; I don't know;
I hear that every answer's No,
But can't believe it can be so.

Hope Is the Thing with Feathers

Emily Dickinson

Hope is the thing with feathers
That perches in the soul,
And sings the tune without the words,
And never stops at all,

And sweetest in the gale is heard;
And sore must be the storm
That could abash the little bird
That kept so many warm.

I've heard it in the chillest land,
And on the strangest sea;
Yet, never, in extremity,
It asked a crumb of me.

Quintrain

Said 'Aql

Once . . . I heard a bird,
an absorbed, ecstatic bird,
eloquently telling
its child: "Fly away,
soar high:
a few bread crumbs
will suffice you,
but the sky
you need . . .
the whole sky."

Acknowledgments and Permissions

The editors are greatly indebted to the following individuals and organizations for their suggestions and assistance in developing this anthology: Sandra Alcosser, Mary Jo Bang, Joshua Beckman, Robert Bly, Marilyn Chin, Cathleen Calbert, Henri Cole, Michael Cóllier, Billy Collins, Robbie Deveney, Greg Djanikian, Rita Dove, Denise Duhamel, Beth Ann Fennelly, Rachel Galvin, Joy Harjo, Brenda Hillman, Tony Hoagland, Paul Hoover, Fanny Howe, Susan Howe, Andrew Hudgins, Lorna Jaffe, Mark Jarman, Suji Kwock Kim, Susan Kinsolving, Henry Labalme, Jan Heller Levi, Heather McHugh, Jane Mead, Susan Mitchell, Carol Muske-Dukes, Marilyn Nelson, Molly Peacock, Srikanth Reddy, Michael Ryan, Sherod Santos, Laurie Sheck, Jeff Shotts, Sean Singer, W. D. Snodgrass, Susan Stewart, Arthur Sze, Lyrae Van Clief-Stefanon, Michael Waters, Susan Wheeler, Massimo Young and The Glady Krieble Delmas Foundation.

Mari Evans, excerpt from "I am a Black Woman" from *I am a Black Woman*. Copyright © 1970 by Mari Evans. Reprinted by permission of the author.

Edward Field, from "Magic Words" from *Magic Words*. Copyright © 1989 by Ed Field. Reprinted by permission of the author.

Robert Francis, "Skier" from *Robert Francis: Collected Poems*. Copyright © 1976 by Robert Francis. Reprinted by permission of University of Massachusetts Press.

Robert Francis, "Summons" from *Robert Francis: Collected Poems*. Copyright © 1976 by Robert Francis. Reprinted by permission of University of Massachusetts Press.

Robert Frost, "Nothing Gold Can Stay" from *The Poetry of Robert Frost: The Collected Poems, Complete and Unabridged*. Copyright © 1964, 1967, 1968, 1970, 1973, 1975 by Lesley Frost Ballantine. Reprinted by permission of Henry Holt and Company. Inc.

Nick Flynn, "Cartoon Physics, part 1" from *Some Ether*. Copyright © 2000. Reprinted by permission of Graywolf Press.

Nikki Giovanni, "Prickled Pickles Don't Smile" from *Vacation Time*. Copyright © 1973, 1978, 1980 by Nikki Giovanni. Reprinted by permission of William Morrow, a division of HarperCollins Publishers, Inc.

Thom Gunn, "Considering the Snail" from *Collected Poems*. Copyright © 1995 by Thom Gunn. Reprinted by permission of Farrar, Straus, and Giroux.

Joy Harjo, "Eagle Poem" from *In Mad Love and War*. Copyright © 1990 by Joy Harjo. Reprinted by permission of Wesleyan University Press.

Langston Hughes, "Harlem Night Song" from *The Collected Poems of Langston Hughes*. Copyright © 1994 by The Estate of Langston Hughes. Reprinted by permission of Alfred A. Knopf, a division of Random House, Inc.

Langston Hughes, "Little Old Letter" from *The Collected Poems of Langston Hughes*. Copyright © 1994 by The Estate of Langston Hughes. Reprinted by permission of Alfred A. Knopf, a division of Random House, Inc.

Kenneth Koch, "Variations on a Theme by William Carlos Williams" from *The Collected Poems of Kenneth Koch*. Copyright © 1962 by Kenneth Koch. Reprinted by permission of Alfred A. Knopf, a division of Random House, Inc.

Ted Kooser, "At the End of the Weekend" from *Sure Signs, New and Selected Poems*. Copyright © 1980 by Ted Kooser. Reprinted by permission of the University of Pittsburgh Press.

Ted Kooser, "Skater" from *Delights & Shadows*. Copyright © 2004 by Ted Kooser. Reprinted by permission of Copper Canyon Press.

Carl Lindner, "First Love" was originally published in *Cottonwood* Issue 33. Reprinted by permission of the author.

Archibald MacLeish, "Ars Poetica" from *Collected Poems 1917–1982*. Copyright © 1985 by The Estate of Archibald MacLeish. Reprinted by permission of Houghton Mifflin Company. All rights reserved.

James McAuley, "Childhood Morning–Homebush" from *Collected Poems 1936–1970*. Copyright © 1971 by James McAuley. Reprinted by permission of HarperCollins Publishers, Inc.

W. S. Merwin, "The Unwritten" from *Migration, New & Selected Poems*. Copyright © 2005 by W. S. Merwin. Reprinted by permission of the Wylie Agency.

Eve Merriam, "How to Eat a Poem" from *Jamboree, Rhymes for All Times*. Copyright © 1962, 1964, 1966, 1973, 1984 by Eve Merriam. Reprinted by permission of Marian Reiner.

Alphabetical Index of Poets, Titles and First Lines

Titles, in italics, are given only when distinct from first lines.

Your First Aquarium

JAY F. HEMDAL

Your First Aquarium

Project Team
Editor: Shari Horowitz
Copy Editor: Tsing Mui
Indexer: Elizabeth Walker
Design Concept: Leah Lococo Ltd.,
 Stephanie Krautheim
Design Layout: Mary Ann Kahn

TFH Publications®
President/CEO: Glen S. Axelrod
Executive Vice President: Mark E. Johnson
Editor-in-Chief: Albert Connelly, Jr.
Production Manager: Kathy Bontz

TFH Publications, Inc.®
One TFH Plaza
Third and Union Avenues
Neptune City, NJ 07753

Printed and bound in China.
14 15 16 17   1 3 5 7 9 8 6 4 2

Library of Congress Cataloging-in-Publication Data
Hemdal, Jay F., 1959-
  Your first aquarium / Jay F. Hemdal.
     pages cm
  Includes index.
  ISBN 978-0-7938-3799-1 (alk. paper)
  1. Aquariums 2. Aquarium fishes. I. Title.
  SF457.3.H463 2014
  639.34--dc23
                    2012035990

The Leader in Responsible Animal Care for Over 50 Years!®

www.tfh.com

Table of Contents

Chapter 1

An Introduction to

Aquariums

You've seen beautiful aquariums in people's homes, pet stores, office lobbies, or restaurants, and now you want to have one of your own. The aquarium hobby will provide you and your family with hours of fascination and relaxation. Before you start, you may need to go "back to school" for a moment. This chapter outlines the history of aquarium keeping, as well as the basic chemistry and biology knowledge required to properly operate your aquarium.

What Is an Aquarium?

In its simplest term, an aquarium (sometimes called a *tank*) is just a container that holds water and aquatic animals. Most aquariums have a clear horizontal pane facing into the water to see the animals more clearly. In addition, all aquariums need some form of life support system to keep the animals alive, like a spaceship has for astronauts.

Home aquariums come in all different shapes and sizes, from tiny ½-gallon (2-liter) bowls to 300-gallon (1135-liter) monsters. Most aquariums have lights to illuminate the fish in the water, heaters with thermostats to keep a stable water temperature, and filters to keep the water quality high so the fish remain healthy. Finally, every aquarium needs a human being to keep everything running smoothly—and that person is you!

Why Aquariums as a Hobby?

Keeping fish in aquariums has proven to be incredibly popular with people for more than 150 years. Goldfish were even kept in bowls long before then in Asia. People keep fish in their homes for a variety of reasons: as "living decorations," for their children's education, for their own amusement, to collect rare specimens, or to raise fish to sell to others. One study at Purdue University showed that elderly people in a nursing home who kept an aquarium had lower stress and were generally happier. Many medical offices have aquariums in their waiting rooms. These tanks have been shown to distract and soothe people stressed about their visit.

A Fascination for Fish

I don't really remember my first aquarium. I was told by my parents that a neighbor gave me two goldfish in a bowl when I was three years old. At the time, I was much more interested in dinosaurs than fish. When I later learned what *extinct* meant and that I would never, ever see a live dinosaur, I became focused on aquariums instead. My first real aquarium was a 10-gallon metal-framed freshwater aquarium that sat on our kitchen counter. My job was to feed the fish and change the water when needed. My father would take me to pet stores on the weekends so I could pick out new fish for the tank. I received a 15-gallon marine (saltwater) aquarium as a birthday gift when I was in the third grade. I recall that my first animal for that tank was a small brown starfish. From that point on, I was truly hooked and have worked with aquariums all my life.

Aquariums can be a life-long career, a passing fad, or anything in between. Hopefully you'll find the information in this book helpful in reaching your goal in the fascinating hobby of home aquariums.

Beautiful aquariums have a relaxing and soothing effect on observers.

The aquarium hobby is an entertaining and relaxing pastime for the entire family. Aquariums are fun to watch, just like television. The fish are beautiful, and aquariums can resemble artwork. Tanks can also be interactive, like video games. But aquariums are really different because they contain living animals that are unpredictable. Aquariums teach people the responsibility of caring for a pet. The animals in an aquarium can show you things about their habits that you would otherwise be unable to see unless you went scuba diving underwater. Aquariums are also challenging; you'll have to design a life support system, your fish may develop a disease, or you may need to figure out how to best feed a particular animal.

There are three important virtues found in all successful aquarium hobbyists. The first is patience.

Rushing into the purchase of a new fish or adding fish to an aquarium too soon is a sure road to disaster. Common sense is also important. For instance, if something about a fish doesn't look right to you, don't ignore it. Stop and think what could be wrong and how serious the problem might be. If there is a serious problem, chances are that it can be corrected by prompt action on your part. Finally, perseverance is also essential. Every aquarium hobbyist loses a fish from time to time. You must learn from your mistakes, and with time, your losses will become minimal. The aquarium hobby will then become a more pleasant experience that you can devote as much or as little time to as you decide.

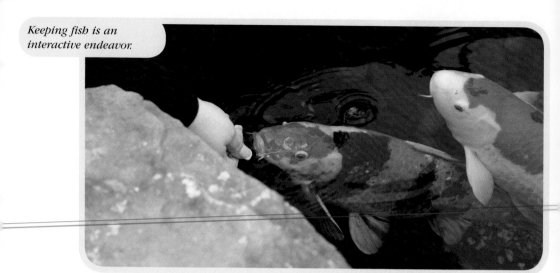

Keeping fish is an interactive endeavor.

Aquariums Past, Present, and Future

Remember, "Those who ignore the past are doomed to repeat it." You don't want to re-learn the solutions to aquarium problems that people before you have already figured out years before. With that in mind, you should take a few minutes to study this history of aquariums and see where the future may lie.

The Past

People actually began keeping fish in captivity as a way to keep their food fresh. Long before the days of refrigerators, food would often spoil. Keeping fish alive in ponds and tanks allowed ancient people to have fresh fish to eat throughout the year. It is thought that over 1000 years ago in China, some of these fish kept for food had brighter colors than the other fish. The people noticed these special fish and kept them alive instead of eating them. Through the process of selective breeding (choosing the offspring that look the way you want them to, and then repeating the process over and

Goldfish were among the first fish kept in captivity.

The Myth of the Balanced Aquarium

Electrical aerators, filters, and heaters had not yet been invented in the 1800s, so fish had to survive in captivity without them. The idea of the balanced aquarium was that if an aquarium was filled with live plants, snails, and just a few fish, it would reach a balance just like ponds and lakes do in nature. The thought was that when they breathe, fish give off carbon dioxide that the plants can then use during photosynthesis. The plants in turn give off oxygen needed by the fish. The snails ate the plants, and then the fish would eat the snails.

Although this was a nice theory, these aquariums were not truly balanced. The reason that they worked at all was that very few fish were ever added to the tank. The water still needed to be changed often, and great care had to be taken not to overstock the tank or all of the fish would soon die. However, unseen to these early aquarium hobbyists were populations of bacteria that lived on the rocks and gravel in these aquariums. These bacteria were very important because they actually convert fish wastes into non-toxic chemicals. Without these important bacteria, the water would have become polluted within a few days. We still use these important beneficial bacteria to help keep our aquarium water clean to this day (read more about *the nitrogen cycle* later on in this chapter).

over), the Chinese developed what we now know as fancy goldfish. These fish were eventually kept in bowls so their beauty could be admired in homes. Around the year 1700, some of these goldfish were sent to Europe. By 1870, goldfish were commonly seen for sale in the United States. This was probably the start of what we now call the aquarium hobby. Some species of fish are beautiful in their wild form, even without selective breeding. People noticed this and began keeping them in bowls of water as well. This brought about the idea of a *balanced aquarium.*

Before the time of electricity, some people tried to heat their aquariums using a small candle set beneath the steel bottom of the aquarium. During this time, filters and aerators ran from hand-driven air pumps or tanks of compressed air. Once most homes had electricity in the early twentieth century, all sorts of aquarium devices were invented: thermostatically controlled heaters, filters, lights, and air pumps. Explorers traveled the world and began bringing home colorful tropical fish back home with them.

After World War II, air travel made it much easier to ship tropical fish back home, and tropical fish farms began to be built in Southern Florida. In the 1960s, marine aquariums became popular, but these fish were difficult

An Introduction to Aquariums

to keep alive at that time because not enough was known about their needs. Like what had been done with goldfish before, selective breeding was used to develop new color varieties of guppies, bettas, angelfish, and many other species. In the 1990s to the present day, interest has grown in *miniature reef aquariums*. These complicated marine aquariums attempt to recreate a tiny section of living reef, right in your own home.

The Present

Now is a great time to be an aquarium hobbyist. The quality of aquarium equipment has never been better. In the old days, such equipment would often break down, harming the fish. With new engineering techniques, aquarium equipment is more energy efficient, lasts longer, and is less expensive. Much more is known about the dietary

needs of fish, and there are new drugs available to help treat fish diseases. Best of all, with overnight delivery services, shipping fish is easier than ever.

In recent years, forced crossbreeding of unrelated species, chemical treatment of developing eggs, and genetic splicing have resulted in the creation of bizarre fish that have never been seen in nature. Examples of these include purple parrot cichlids, hybrid giant catfish, and GloFish® (zebrafish that have jellyfish genes spliced into their own genetic code). Some aquarium hobby purists hate these "freaks," but others find them fascinating. The only real problem is that some of these fish are painted with chemicals to make them look the way they do. This process can harm the fish's delicate skin. Besides, the colors

Parrot cichlids are hybrids that have been created through cross-breeding two different species of fish.

of these dyed fish soon fade away, so it is best to avoid buying them.

The Future

People are increasingly disconnected from the natural world. When I was a child, I spent every summer day in the woods or down at a nearby creek looking at animals. Nowadays, people spend more time indoors. They don't see nature up close, and this may lead to them not caring as much about the natural world. One way to reconnect is to bring nature home to you, with an aquarium.

Most freshwater fish are unable to tolerate a high concentration of salt in their water.

Aquariums can be one of the best ways for people to learn about nature, but they do take time, and people seem to be very busy these days. Still, it often pays to make time for fun activities like aquariums. So, turn off the television, unplug the video game console, and spend some time with your aquariums. You'll learn a lot about nature and biology, and you can continue in the long tradition of home aquarium fishkeeping!

Basic Aquarium Science: Chemistry

This book strives to explain the aquarium hobby from a relatively simple, non-technical standpoint. Still, a basic of knowledge of such topics as chemistry, biology, and physics is necessary for the reader to fully understand some of the more complex aquarium topics. The following section gives you this basic information.

Water

Water is a chemical compound with the formula H_2O. A molecule of water contains one oxygen and two hydrogen atoms attached to one another by chemical bonds. Liquid water is obviously the most important requirement for fish, but water can also exist as a solid (ice) or a gas (water vapor). Water covers 71 percent of the Earth's surface and is needed by all forms of life. Less than one percent of all water on Earth is found as fresh water in ponds, lakes, and rivers. The rest of the water is found in the oceans, which are filled with water that contains different types of salts at a concentration of 3.5 percent. Brackish water is found where freshwater rivers mix with the ocean. The salt content of brackish water varies from one half to three percent. Different species of fish have different salt content needs. For example, most freshwater fish cannot live in the salty ocean.

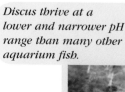

Discus thrive at a lower and narrower pH range than many other aquarium fish.

In addition, water must be at the proper temperature for fish to live. Most tropical fish species kept in home aquariums do best when kept at a temperature range of around 75° to 80°F (24° to 27° Celsius). Some fish, such as goldfish, can tolerate water temperatures as low as 34°F (1°C).

pH

In the simplest terms, the pH (always written little p, capital H) measurement tells the aquarist how basic or acidic an aquarium's water is. Most freshwater aquariums have an optimum pH range of 6.5 to 7.5. Many fish can do well in an even wider range, but a few fish species have a more narrow pH range.

A water molecule is composed of two hydrogen atoms and one oxygen atom. Some of these water molecules separate into ions, in the manner that occurs when salts are dissolved in water. The pH is simply a measurement of the concentration of hydrogen ions present in a sample of water. The pH scale is logarithmic, with lower pH measurements having a greater concentration of hydrogen ions. At a pH of 8.0, there are 1/10 the number

Some pH test kits require you to add a few drops of a liquid reagent to a sample of aquarium water.

of hydrogen ions that there is in water with a pH of 7.0 (a pH of 7.0, called neutral, is neither acidic or basic).

Organic acids given off by fish as wastes tend to cause a drop in the pH of the water over time. This can best be corrected by doing routine partial water changes, which dilute the concentrations of these acidic wastes. A less effective method would be to counteract the effects of acids by the addition of a base or buffer to raise the pH. The reasons why this is a less effective method to maintain a proper pH is that there are other waste products that build up in aquarium water aside from those that drive the pH down. The best means to remove these is by the diluting effect of partial water changes.

Measuring the pH in aquariums is a relatively simple matter. There are many inexpensive test kits available from pet stores that will do this job. For most routine testing, a pH test kit that can make measurements in the range of 6.0 to 8.5 is best.

Dissolved Gases

Gases from the air dissolve into an aquarium's water in different amounts, depending on the temperature of the water, the amount of aeration, and the type of gas involved. Aquarium animals have definite requirements for levels of most dissolved gases. It is very expensive and probably not worthwhile for the home aquarist to directly measure the concentration of these gases in their home aquariums. Luckily, there are ways to make sure that dissolved gases are maintained at the proper levels using the life support equipment attached to the aquarium.

Oxygen

Oxygen (two oxygen atoms bonded together, written as O_2) is perhaps the most important of these dissolved gases in terms of the health of aquarium animals. Most fish get their oxygen directly from the water through their gills (although some, such as lungfish, can breathe air at the surface). Proper

Some specialized fish, such as lungfish, can breathe oxygen directly from the air.

Aeration not only adds oxygen to the water, it drives off unwanted carbon dioxide.

Careful with Gases

All gases naturally found in air are dissolved in the water of an aquarium as well. Naturally occurring gases such as argon, xenon, and the like are also present, but they are of no concern for the health of the fish. Artificially introduced gases can be a problem for home aquariums. These are fumes and gases from household products such as paint, pest sprays, smoking, and the like. Needless to say, never introduce any of these gases into a room containing an aquarium if there is any chance they might be harmful and if the air pump or filter might pick them up and dissolve them in the aquarium's water.

levels of this gas must be dissolved in the water to keep the animals healthy. The higher the salt level or temperature, the less oxygen can be dissolved in the water.

Aeration or the act of passing air bubbles through the aquarium's water is the most important way to keep the amount of dissolved oxygen at proper levels. The bubbles themselves do not add much oxygen to the water, but as the bubbles rise to the surface, they carry water with them. This water has been depleted of oxygen by the respiration of the beneficial bacteria and the fish. When this water contacts the air above the tank, it picks up new oxygen. Water circulation from pumps also helps in the same fashion, as long as the pumps are moving water from the bottom of the aquarium to the top

and not horizontally through the tank. Keeping the aquarium water at the proper temperature, aerating and circulating it well, and not overcrowding the tank with fish all help keep dissolved oxygen levels within the proper range.

Carbon Dioxide

Carbon dioxide (one carbon atom and two oxygen atoms, written as CO_2) is a gas given off by living organisms as a product of their respiration, whether it is from the animals in an aquarium, or the beneficial bacteria (more about this later). If carbon dioxide levels build up in the water, the fish will begin breathing (using their gills) faster than normal and may eventually die. While aeration adds oxygen to the water by bringing the water to the surface where it can pick up oxygen, the same aeration drives away excess carbon dioxide by breaking the surface tension of the water. This is hard to understand until you think of a carbonated can of soda—shaking it up drives off the carbon dioxide that gives it its fizz.

Nitrogen Gas

Nitrogen gas (N_2) is the most abundant gas in our atmosphere, but it is relatively inert and has little effect on aquarium animals. Plants need nitrogen for proper growth, but most use other sources such as ammonia and nitrate rather than the gas itself. In some rare situations, excess nitrogen can be dissolved in aquarium water and can cause a problem with the fish, similar to how scuba divers get the bends. Luckily, aeration helps to drive off excess dissolved nitrogen just as it does with carbon dioxide.

Dissolved Solids

Dissolved solids is a measure of the amount of non-organic compounds dissolved in water. Most of these compounds are different types of salts. As mentioned, marine aquariums have a high amount of salts dissolved in their water. Freshwater aquariums have much less. However, freshwater fish cannot survive if there are no dissolved solids at all in their water. Pure (distilled or deionized) water has little, if any, dissolved solids in it, so freshwater fish cannot survive in this type of water. As mentioned, they require a particular amount of dissolved solids to thrive. Luckily, the tap water in most regions of the world contains sufficient amounts of these compounds to meet the needs of most fish.

One type of dissolved solids that is important to measure is the calcium hardness level. Some freshwater fish prefer *soft* water, which has very little calcium in it. Other fish, such as some African cichlids, prefer water that has much more calcium dissolved in it, and this is called *hard* water. Most freshwater fishes do fine in water that is neither too soft nor overly hard. If you have a water softener on

Adding gravel from an established aquarium can help jump-start the nitrogen cycle.

the water supply to your home, you may want to focus on keeping fish that prefer soft water, or you may want to bypass the water softener when you fill your aquarium.

Dissolved Organic Compounds

The term "organic compound" may not mean the same thing to different people. To a chemist, it means certain carbon-containing chemical compounds. To a biologist, it might mean any compound produced by a living organism. To a home aquarist, it may mean a combination of these definitions. Home aquarists generally use the term *organic waste* to describe any toxic chemical produced as a byproduct of a living animal, found at higher concentrations in an aquarium than it would in natural waters. These organic compounds build up in aquarium water over time as the animals eat food and excrete wastes.

The filtration system removes some of these wastes, but others must be removed by performing partial water changes.

Freshwater aquariums that have overly high levels of these compounds will have a low pH and look distinctly yellow when compared to distilled or tap water. Organic chemicals can accidently be added to aquarium water, and this in turn may harm the fish. The best way to avoid accidental poisoning of aquariums is always be aware of any way a chemical compound could be added to the aquarium by chance. Before you reach into a tank, ask yourself, "Are my hands clean of all soaps, perfumes, and other chemicals? Are there no strong odors in the room, which might mean that my air pump is injecting some chemical into the aquarium's water? Are the decorations I want to use in the tank safe for aquarium use?" If one can answer yes to all these questions, the chance of accidental poisoning is greatly diminished.

The Nitrogen Cycle

Protein in the food you feed to your fish contains nitrogen compounds. Excess food can decompose, and fish digest the food they eat. Both processes release the nitrogen compound known as ammonia, and this can be toxic to fish. In natural waters, the animal density is so low that these waste products never build up to toxic levels. The fish in home aquariums are always much more crowded than in nature. Nitrogenous wastes can build up in the water and must be removed before they reach concentrations lethal to the fish.

Water changes would work to dilute these wastes, but most aquarists also rely on a process called *biological filtration*. This term describes the populations of helpful bacteria that grow naturally in aquariums (often living on the gravel or on the filter material). These bacteria use the ammonia produced by the fish as a food source. These bacteria get food energy from the ammonia, and then they produce another compound, called nitrite, as their own waste product. Nitrite is not as deadly to fish as ammonia, but it can still be a problem. Luckily, there is a second species of bacteria that converts the nitrite to the much less toxic compound known as nitrate. As long as

Home aquariums are more densely populated than natural water bodies, which is one of the reasons nitrogenous waste levels can build up to potentially lethal levels.

New Tank Syndrome

Pet stores are very familiar with something called *"new tank syndrome."* This happens when a beginning aquarium hobbyist rushes out and buys too many fish and adds them all at once to a newly set up aquarium. New aquarium keepers almost always overfeed their fish. When you combine the ammonia waste being produced by a large number of fish with no beneficial bacteria present, and too much food added to the tank, the ammonia level quickly rises to dangerous levels.

Many beginning aquarium keepers don't know how to test their new aquarium's water. The result is that the fish start to suffer from ammonia poisoning. The fish become listless and stop eating, and may die. Sometimes, in extreme cases, every fish in the tank will die. The beginning aquarium keeper then either drains the tank in frustration, or adds a new group of fish. Very often, if they do add a new group of fish, the bacteria that manage the nitrogen cycle have had time to become established, and the second group of fish does just fine. The new aquarium keeper often just decides that the first fish died from some unknown problem, never even knowing that it could have been easily prevented.

these bacterial populations are healthy, the tank is not overcrowded and regular water changes are made, these dissolved waste products won't reach levels harmful to the fish. This process is termed the nitrogen cycle.

How to Establish the Nitrogen Cycle of an Aquarium

While the beneficial bacteria grow naturally in a new aquarium, it is a process that does take from 4 to 12 weeks to become fully operational. There are two periods of time where the nitrogenous waste levels of ammonia and nitrite can rise above the danger point for the fish. These levels can be measured using ammonia and nitrite test kits (make sure the ones you buy are designed for use in freshwater aquariums). Because you do not need to test the water every day during this process, you may find it more economical to have your local pet store test your water for a small fee.

The best way to establish the nitrogen cycle in a new freshwater aquarium is to add a handful of gravel or filter material from an established tank before adding any fish. There are also live bacteria products on the market that can serve the same function—check with your pet store. Once the bacteria has been added, you can start by adding a few very hardy fish and then wait for two weeks, and add a couple more. Repeating this process of gradually adding new fish to the aquarium ensures that the ammonia and nitrite spikes never get high enough to reach the danger zone.

Fish can feel vibrations in the water using their lateral line.

Should there be an unexpected spike in ammonia or nitrite, there are chemicals that you can add to the water to help detoxify these compounds. In addition, ammonia is much less toxic to fish at a low pH, and nitrite is partially detoxified by the presence of a small amount of salt in the water (1 teaspoon per gallon).

Basic Aquarium Science: Biology

The majority of living things kept by freshwater aquarium keepers are species of vertebrates known as fish. Some aquariums do house live plants and a few have animals without backbones known as invertebrates, but it is the fish that most people are interested in. The better you understand the biology of the animals living in your care, the better you can meet their needs and keep them alive and healthy.

The scientific study of fish is called ichthyology. A typical fish has gills to extract oxygen from the water, fins to help propel it through the water.

The skin of most fishes is scaled, and most are considered *ectotherms* (cold blooded), which means they cannot regulate their body temperature. Most fish lay eggs, but some, such as guppies and mollies, give birth to live young.

SMALL FRY

Do Fish Go to School?

Some species of fish exhibit a fascinating behavior where they swim together in groups. Commonly called a *school*, this is done for a variety of reasons: protection against predators, to find a mate, or even to increase swimming efficiency. Scientists also use the term *shoal* for some of these groups of fish, depending on why the group was formed.

Fish with down-turned mouths, such as catfish, eat food off the bottom.

There are over 28,000 species of fish known to science: 27,000 bony fish, 970 sharks and rays, plus about 108 species of jawless fishes (the hagfish and lampreys). About 40 percent of this number (about 10,000 species) is fish that are found for at least part of their lives in freshwater. There are fish that spend some of their time on land, such as mudskippers. Others, like cavefish, are totally blind. Fish live in the highest mountain streams and in the depths of the oceans. There is even an eel that is a parasite and lives inside the hearts of large sharks. Fish range in size from the tiny 1/3-inch-long (8-mm) stout infantfish to the gigantic 52-foot-long (16-meter) whale shark.

Most fish have good eyesight, plus they have a way to feel vibrations in the water using special skin cells along their *lateral line*. Because a fish in an aquarium has nowhere to really hide, try to avoid sudden movements outside the aquarium or loud vibrations (such as a small child pounding on the side of the tank) that would cause

the fish to become frightened. People have questioned if fish can feel pain or not. Some scientists believe they can, while others disagree. The problem may never be answered because there is no way for us to truly understand if fish are aware enough to feel pain like mammals do. Since nobody knows for sure, you should always assume that they can feel pain, and treat your fish with respect as you should every living thing.

The shape of a fish's mouth can tell you a lot about the fish. Fish with large mouths are obviously adapted to feeding on large prey items (maybe other fish!). A fish with a down-turned mouth is designed for feeding from the bottom. Some fish have upturned mouths, and they prefer floating food. Some fish have scraping mouths that they use to rasp algae off of rocks and other surfaces in the aquarium. Catfish have whiskers that they use to sense nearby food—even in cloudy water, or at night.

Most fish have fins (which can be paired or unpaired), and these are given specific names based on their location. The basic shape of the caudal (tail) fin can sometimes be used to predict the behavior of a fish in an aquarium. Fish, such as rainbowfish with lunate (moon-shaped) caudal fins

What's in a Name?

Is it *fish* or *fishes*? *Fish* is used when speaking about one fish, or a group of fish in a particular location: "That *fish* was the largest *fish* in the aquarium." *Fishes* is used when referring to multiple species: "The *fishes* of the world..."

Each species of fish is given a "Latinized binomial" by scientists, which is a fish's scientific name. This is usually written in two parts, *Genus species*. Written in italics, only the genus name is capitalized. A few organisms have a subspecies name, and this is written as a third word, after species. There can be only one valid scientific name for a fish, and no two fish can share the same valid scientific name. As scientific names change, the old ones are referred to as *synonyms*. Remember that scientific names are the same no matter what language is being spoken, so they are the best way for people in different countries to be certain they are talking about the same species.

A single species of fish may have a variety of common names. The common bluegill also goes by the name bream, brim, roach, stumpknocker, and copper belly. However, it has only one scientific name: *Lepomis macrochirus*. Because of the confusion surrounding fish with multiple common names, the American Fisheries Society and the FishBase website have settled on a single common name in English for each species of fish.

Mistakes happen: The palette surgeonfish, kept by marine aquarists, goes by a huge variety of common names in just the English language alone. The most popular in the aquarium trade is "hippo tang," which is derived from a mispronunciation of its species name, "*hepatus*," that reminds people of the word "hippopotamus." Enough people were confused that way, and the name stuck. Other very common misnomers with aquariums include "tubiflex" for "tubifex," "chiclets" for "cichlids," and "shrimp-brine" for "brine shrimp."

Remember that there is really no "right" or "wrong" common name – as long as people know which species you're referring to when you talk about it, then the name you used is just fine.

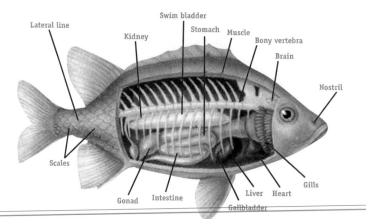

Lateral line
Kidney
Swim bladder
Stomach
Muscle
Bony vertebra
Brain
Nostril
Scales
Gonad
Intestine
Liver
Heart
Gills
Gallbladder

and most fish have a swim bladder. Gills are very delicate structures located below and behind the fish's eyes. Blood flows through the gill filaments and gathers oxygen from the water as the fish opens and closes its mouth. The swim bladder has gas in it that allows the fish to float in mid water. If this structure is damaged by disease, the fish may float at the surface or sink to the bottom.

are typically fast swimmers that cannot turn very well. Fish with squared-off tails, such as discus, are slower but more maneuverable. Fish with soft, rounded caudal fins, such as killifish, are very slow swimmers but highly maneuverable.

Internally, fish are not all that different from other vertebrate animals. They have a brain, heart, liver, stomach, reproductive organs, and kidneys. The main difference is that fish have gills

Putting Everything Together

After reading the information in this chapter about water chemistry, the nitrogen cycle, and fish biology, you can see how they all come together by studying figure 1.1. This diagram outlines how all of these factors

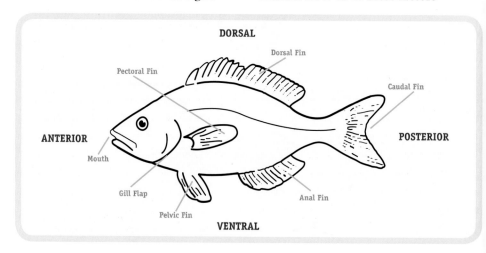

DORSAL

Dorsal Fin

Pectoral Fin

Caudal Fin

ANTERIOR

POSTERIOR

Mouth

Gill Flap

Anal Fin

Pelvic Fin

VENTRAL

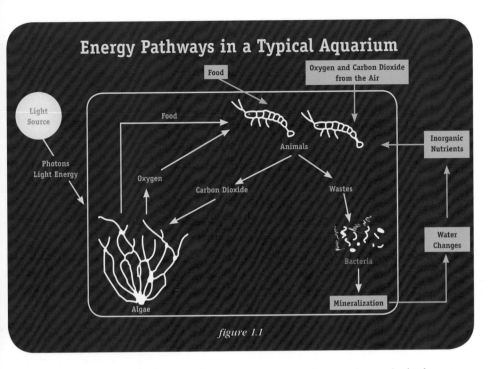

Energy Pathways in a Typical Aquarium

Food

Oxygen and Carbon Dioxide from the Air

Light Source

Food

Animals

Photons Light Energy

Oxygen

Carbon Dioxide

Wastes

Inorganic Nutrients

Bacteria

Water Changes

Algae

Mineralization

figure 1.1

interact. Try following the lines with the arrows to see how changes in your aquarium influence other factors. Some of the arrows are very simple, while others are more complex. Without the arrow showing food going into the aquarium, your animals may die. Without beneficial bacteria, the waste levels will climb.

Aeration is vital in keeping the carbon dioxide and oxygen in balance between the air and the water. If too much light enters the aquarium, algae may grow out of control, faster than the fish can eat it, and this looks unsightly. If you do not perform proper water changes, the mineralized waste products (nitrate in particular) will build up, causing harm to the animals. Some pathways are not shown; if

your aquarium springs a leak, the water drains out and all of the related pathways stop working! If a fish dies and is not removed, its body tissues then become waste, and there may not be enough bacteria present to mineralize them, and the water will become polluted. Likewise, if you add too many fish to an aquarium, the waste levels climb, while the dissolved oxygen concentration drops to an unhealthy level.

If you understand all of the pathways in figure 1.1 and make sure they never get out of balance, you will always be more successful with your aquariums! This holistic approach to aquariums will enable you to truly understand the science that goes on in your tank.

An Introduction to Aquariums

Chapter 2

A Place to Stay:

Aquariums and Equipment

Even before you decide on what species of fish you want to keep, you need to choose the size of the aquarium you want and what equipment you'll need in order to operate it. This chapter describes the different aquariums and equipment that are available to home aquarium keepers.

The aquarium and all its equipment are called a *life support system*, and your fish will rely on this to keep them alive and healthy. You don't want to cut corners when purchasing this equipment—if it fails, it usually means a big problem for the fish.

You may find that after selecting all the equipment you need, your local pet store can put together a package deal for you. Some stores discount the price of a complete setup, while others may offer you a discount on future fish purchases.

One thing is certain; you need to have the aquarium operating properly *before* buying any fish. Fish cannot wait in their plastic transport bags while you assemble all of the aquarium equipment, adjust the water temperature, and then dechlorinate the water.

Tank Selection and Placement

The first, most basic decision you need to make is what size aquarium you are interested in. The answer of "the biggest aquarium you can afford" doesn't really help because the tank itself is only part of the cost of an operating aquarium. You should first look at the fish choices in chapter three and choose an aquarium large enough to house the fish you are interested in

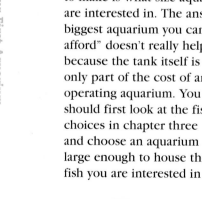

The aquarium itself and all the equipment in it are known as the life support system for your fish.

keeping (allowing room for them to grow of course!).

Tank Size

The most common size for a first aquarium is probably a 10-gallon tank. These are inexpensive and readily available, but they may not be the best choice because new aquarium keepers almost always overstock these small tanks. You may find that a 29-gallon tank 30 inches long by 12 inches wide by 18 inches deep, (76 cm x 30 cm x 46 cm) is a good compromise between a larger size, while still being relatively affordable in price. In recent years, *nano* or micro aquariums have become popular. Some of these only hold a few gallons of water. These small tanks are almost a hobby unto themselves, and you should probably gain some experience operating a full-sized aquarium before trying one of these diminutive tanks. Aquariums that are very tall and narrow may not have enough surface area to allow for

Selecting Your Pet Store

Finding a good pet store to buy your equipment and fish from is very important. Not only does the store need to offer high quality equipment and healthy fish, they need to serve as an informational resource for you if you have questions. Selecting a good store is not just a matter of low price, how large the store is, or how close it is to your home. Other factors to consider include the following:

Is their store clean and well stocked? This is a sign of a flourishing business, and that means that other customers have found them to be a good store to shop at.

Are there dead fish in the tanks? Every pet store will lose fish, sometimes quite a few of them (fish arriving from delayed flights, or that are sick, for example). However, a store that does not remove these fish promptly is not showing very much pride in their work.

Are there employees available to answer your questions? The clerk waiting on you may not be able to answer your questions, but they should be able to find another employee who can.

Do they stand behind their fish's health? Most stores will guarantee their fish for a certain length of time, as long as you follow their advice. Stores that offer no guarantee may be selling poorer quality stock.

Price is important to a point, but remember that if the store offers you good information, there is value in that as well.

Mail-order and online fish stores have become very popular, and some offer very good service. However, beginning aquarists are usually not well enough informed to buy products (especially live fish), without first seeing the item and being able to ask questions and compare options.

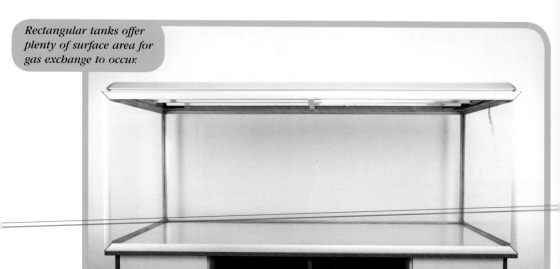

Rectangular tanks offer plenty of surface area for gas exchange to occur.

proper gas exchange, so beginners are advised to avoid novelty aquariums like that and opt for one in a more standard, rectangular form.

It is often said that small tanks are less stable than large ones, and that changes in water quality can happen so fast in a small tank that you don't have much time to correct the problem. This is often used as the reason to buy a larger aquarium. Actually, there is nothing about a small tank that makes it less stable, as long as the weight (mass) of fish per gallon of water is the same as with a larger tank. This is called the *bioload* of an aquarium. Two grams of fish in a 2-gallon tank will be just as stable as 10 grams of fish in a 10-gallon tank, or 100 grams in a 100-gallon tank—they all contain 1 gram of fish mass per gallon. These three examples will all require proportionally the same

amount of food, and their filters (if sized properly) will be able to handle the fish wastes given off to the same degree. Why then does everyone seem to just *know* that smaller aquariums are less stable? The real reason for this is simply because it is so much easier to overcrowd a smaller aquarium. Adding a 2-gram fish to the 100-gallon aquarium in this example only increases its bio-load by 2 percent, while adding that same 2-gram fish to a 2-gallon aquarium would double the bio-load!

Tank Shape

The next question you need to answer is what shape your aquarium will be. Most standard aquariums are rectangles, a bit longer than they are tall or wide. However, there are many other shapes available that you might find more attractive or will fit your home décor better. Multi-sided tanks are popular; usually these are hexagon shaped, some with elongated sides facing the center of the room. These, as well as cylinder tanks, are useful in areas where the aquarium is going to viewed from all sides. Bowfront tanks are increasingly popular. They are a standard rectangular tank with the front viewing window bowed out somewhat. Corner bowfront tanks are great for fitting tightly into the corner of a room. Remember that too many seams in an aquarium may obscure the view of the fish, and cylinders and bubble shapes will cause weird visual distortions of the fish as they swim past.

Placement

Once you have a rough idea of the size and shape of aquarium you are interested in, you need to think about proper placement of the aquarium.

Water weighs about 8.4 pounds per gallon (1 kilogram per liter). Add to that the weight of the decorations, gravel, and the tank itself, and a 10-gallon aquarium may end up weighing 100 pounds (45.4 kg). A very large home aquarium can be like trying to park a small car in your living room! You need to be certain that the support stand you choose can handle this weight and that the floor in your home can as well. The safest aquarium stands to use are those that are built for that purpose. Never try to place a filled aquarium on household furniture and only build your own stand if you are comfortable that you know what you are doing. Some apartment complexes have a limit to the size of aquarium you can have (in case it springs a leak and floods the tenants on the floor below you). You should also make sure that your home

An aquarium that is full of water is extremely heavy and requires a stand built for the purpose of supporting it.

Water, Water Everywhere, But Not a Drop to Drink!

You need to consider what water source you will use to fill your aquarium.

- Bottled spring water works very well for small freshwater aquariums, but it becomes very expensive if you use it to fill a larger aquarium.
- Distilled water lacks vital minerals and is expensive, so it is best not to use this type of water.
- Rainwater, like distilled water, lacks vital minerals and may also contain air pollution particles, so do not use it.
- Reverse osmosis (R/O) is used to purify some types of well or tap water. It may remove too many minerals and make the water too soft for many fish.
- Tap water is the most convenient, but you will need to dechlorinate it prior to use. Your pet store can inform you of any special concerns they may have about using your tap water.
- Well water has characteristics that vary greatly throughout the world. Check with your local pet store; they will be familiar with the type of well water in your region. If your well has sulfide in it (giving it a rotten egg smell), you will need to aerate it for 24 hours before use. In most cases, it is best to use well water before it goes through the softener or other treatment system.

insurance covers water damage from aquariums.

Placement of the aquarium inside the room is important. Large aquariums should be situated above floor joists, or near a wall. Be careful with any aquarium in homes with small children, as a curious child might try to climb the stand to see the fish better and have the whole tank tip over on them.

Consider the amount of sunlight that will reach the tank from nearby windows. Even a small amount of sunlight entering an aquarium for a few minutes a day will cause unsightly algae growth. Some people suggest that you should avoid placing an aquarium near drafts, but with the thermostatically controlled heaters that most aquariums have, this is not really an issue.

Aquarium Construction

Aquariums can be constructed from a variety of materials, but the most common is an all-glass design, with acrylic (Plexiglas) coming in close second. Glass aquariums tend to give the water a slight greenish hue, and the corner seams (glued with silicone sealant) can be unsightly. There are special glass aquariums that are seamless, and those made of a clearer glass, but these are more expensive. Acrylic aquariums are impact resistant, have stronger seams (they rarely leak), and are more transparent, but they scratch very easily. Some small aquariums are molded from a thin styrene-type plastic that, while inexpensive, tends to shatter if bumped or jarred.

Aquariums set on a stand must be level on all four corners and properly supported along the entire bottom. It may help to utilize some cushioning product such as closed-cell foam between the tank and the stand, as this can help level out small differences in elevation. Some aquarium stands are built with cabinets beneath the tank, and this is a big help in hiding pumps, filters, and other equipment. Just be sure to secure the cabinet doors in households with small children.

Filtration
Types of Filtration

There are many types of filters available for home aquariums. They all use some combination of the following three different methods to maintain a clean, healthy environment for your fish.

Biological filtration: Filters with biological filtration provide a surface for the beneficial bacteria to adhere to, and then pass water over that surface. In this way, the toxic ammonia and nitrates are removed from the water. As mentioned, these bacteria do take time to grow. You also have to be aware that some fish medications can kill these bacteria, and washing the material they are adhering to can rinse them away.

Mechanical filtration: In mechanical filters, particles in the water are trapped by some type of filter material—a sponge, filter floss, or a pleated cartridge. It is important to understand that these particles are not actually removed from the aquarium until you clean the filter media they are trapped in. Some filters work as both biological and mechanical filters at the same time.

Chemical filtration: There are a variety of materials that extract various toxins from the water and can be placed into a filter for the purpose of chemical filtration. Activated carbon removes organic compounds and some metals. Clinoptilolite (a type of zeolite mineral) are white pellets that remove ammonia from freshwater aquariums. If your water is too hard (there is too much dissolved calcium in it), there are water chemical beads that can be used to soften it. Most chemical filters have a drawback in that they can only absorb a certain amount of toxins,

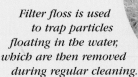

Filter floss is used to trap particles floating in the water, which are then removed during regular cleaning.

Quick-Change Artists?

Most fish have the ability to change their color, at least to a small degree. As a general rule, using light-colored gravel and pale backgrounds or decorations will cause the fish's color to pale considerably, sometimes turning them completely silver or white. Conversely, dark-colored decorations tend to cause the fish's coloration to deepen.

yet there is no easy way to determine when they have become exhausted and need to be changed. In most cases, chemical filtration is used in addition to mechanical filtration to ensure good water quality.

Types of Filters

The simplest filter is perhaps the undergravel. These slotted plastic plates sit out of sight below the gravel layer of the aquarium, with only riser tubes in the back of the tank showing. Air is pumped down the riser tubes where it is released to travel back to the surface. As the air bubbles rise, they carry water with them. This is called an *airlift*. This process moves water and aerates it at the same time. Water that rises up the tubes is replaced by new water flowing down through the gravel. Detritus and other waste is then captured between

the gravel grains. More importantly, beneficial bacteria grow on the surface of the gravel, extracting fish wastes from the water. Cleaning an undergravel filter can be a bit of a chore. The easiest way is to use a siphon cleaning device, and its use is described in chapter 5.

Sponge filters work on the same principle as the undergravel filter: The airlift pulls water through the sponge. The sponge traps detritus and serves as a site for the beneficial bacteria to grow. The problems with these filters are that they are limited in capacity to aquariums holding less than around 20 gallons (76 liters), they take up a lot of space inside the tank, and most people find them unattractive. They do work well for small hospital tanks, however. They need to be cleaned regularly by squeezing them forcefully in a bucket of tank water. If you wash the sponge with tap water, the chlorine will kill many of the beneficial bacteria that these filters rely on to keep the ammonia levels down. Like undergravel filters, a sponge filter needs two or three weeks to be colonized by beneficial bacteria before they begin to work efficiently.

Power filters are very popular with many home aquarists. Most models either hang on the back of the tank or sit beneath the tank with an intake and output hose running up over the side. Power filters use pumps to move water from the tank, through the filter material, and back into the aquarium. The filter material traps large waste particles and provides a site for beneficial bacteria to grow. Many power filters also have a space for chemical filtration compounds such as carbon or a zeolite mineral.

The capacity of power filters is often given in units called GPH, or gallons per hour. Unfortunately, there is no set GPH value for a given size aquarium. Some filters are more efficient than others and may have a low GPH value, yet they are still capable of keeping the aquarium water clean. For the most part, you can use the manufacturer's guidelines in selecting a filter for a particular-sized aquarium. A general rule of thumb is that all of the water in an aquarium should pass through the filter at least three times an hour, so a 50-gallon (187-liter) tank would need a filter that can process at least 150 gallons (568 liters) per hour. It is possible to put too large of a filter on an aquarium. An oversized filter will create strong water currents that the fish will have difficulty swimming against, plus it may even heat up the water too much, especially in the summertime. A filter that can process six times the aquarium's capacity in an hour may be too powerful.

Aeration

As mentioned in chapter one, air bubbles rising up through the water column help aerate it, adding oxygen and driving off excess carbon dioxide. The most economical way to achieve good aeration is through an air pump and airstone. Diaphragm air pumps are relatively inexpensive and are sized by the number of outlets needed, as well as the depth of the water (deeper water creates back pressure that requires a more powerful air pump). Airstones range from single small stones to long air wands or even plastic

Sponge filters offer a surface for beneficial bacteria to grow on and trap particles in the water, but they are only meant for aquariums that are 20 gallons or less.

Power filters can hang off the back of the tank, and many offer mechanical, chemical, and biological filtration.

of the tank and give off between one and two watts of light energy per gallon of water. Tanks with live plants may require double that amount of light.

Some advanced aquarists are also beginning to adopt LED (light-emitting diode) lighting. While these lights are expensive to purchase, they last a lot longer and use less electricity than other lights, so they may be more cost effective in the long run.

Certain fluorescent bulbs (the ones that are pink colored when running) can really make the fish's colors sparkle. Bulbs that are bluer in color reduce the yellow tint sometimes seen in old aquarium water.

Try to avoid turning the aquarium and the room lights on or off at the same time. To avoid stressing the fish due to a sudden change in light levels, it is always best to turn on the room lights first, wait a few minutes, and then turn on the brighter aquarium lights. At night, just reverse the process. Turn off the aquarium lights but leave the room lights on for a few minutes so the fish can prepare to sleep (yes, fish do sleep!).

moving ornaments. The diaphragm of the air pump will need to be replaced every few years, and airstones need to be replaced when they begin to clog. Airline tubing and valves tie the whole system together.

Lighting

Unless your planned aquarium will contain live plants, lighting is an issue primarily for aesthetics (how the tank looks to you). As long as the fish have enough light to see their food (and some, such as catfish, can feed in the dark!), they will be fine. Incandescent light fixtures have almost become a thing of the past—these bulbs produce a lot of waste heat, burn out frequently, and give a yellowish cast to the aquarium's water. Almost all aquarium keepers find that a full hood (to keep the fish from jumping out) fluorescent tube fixture gives the best results. For freshwater aquariums, a fluorescent fixture should span the entire length

Heating

The majority of fish suitable for home aquariums come from tropical regions. This means that their preferred water temperature is warmer than typical room temperature. In addition, the water temperature of their wild habitats changes very slowly, if much at all, over the year, while an unheated aquarium in a home might experience temperature swings of as much as 10°F (5.5°C) throughout a day. For this reason, an aquarium heater, thermostat, and thermometer are required pieces of equipment for a typical home aquarium. In most cases, the heater and thermostat will be built into the same device. Because these heaters are electrical devices that are submerged in water, there is the potential for safety issues. Make sure that the heater you select is either UL or CE registered and that you follow the installation instructions very carefully.

A good-quality thermometer is also required. The most popular kind is an LCD (liquid crystal display) type that sticks to the outside of the tank. These read the water temperature through the glass and change color depending on the temperature. More old fashioned are the glass thermometers with the red alcohol line that are placed inside the aquarium. The level of the red line corresponds to the water temperature.

Aquariums containing live plants require more light than ones that don't.

Safe or Not?

Ceramics: Safe as long as no lead was used in the glaze; clay pots are fine
Coral: A few small pieces would be okay, but may dissolve over time
Driftwood: Only use special aquarium-safe driftwood from a pet store
Glass: Safe as long as there are no sharp edges that could injure the fish
Granite: All hard/dense stones will be safe for use
Metal: Except for objects made from titanium, avoid using metals
Mineral Specimens: Some, such as halite, will dissolve in water, best not to use them
Plastics: Most are safe, but some have anti-mold chemicals added
Sandstone: Too soft, avoid any rock that has iron (rust) streaks in it
Sea Fans: Not safe inside the aquarium, can be used as a backdrop behind the tank
Shells: A few shells are fine; avoid snail shells that may still have tissue inside
Slate: Safe to use, but shale, a similar rock, may not be safe
Sponges (natural): Not safe inside the aquarium, can be used as a backdrop

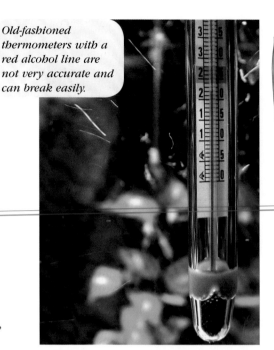

Old-fashioned thermometers with a red alcohol line are not very accurate and can break easily.

These are not very accurate and prone to breakage. There are digital thermometers that sit outside the aquarium and read the water temperature from a probe that hangs in the water. These are usually accurate, but if the probe gets bumped and slides out of the water, it will then start reading the air temperature above the water, and not the water itself—giving you incorrect information.

One trick in selecting an accurate thermometer is to check all of them hanging on the store's display. You'll notice they may not all read the same temperature, yet you know they should because they are all in the same section of the store. Find one that reads in the middle of any range, as that will likely be the most accurate.

Shopping List for a New Aquarium

Aquarium, with an optional decorative background to fit
Stand
Lid with light
Gravel: 1 to 2 pounds per gallon of tank size (.12 to .24 kg / liter tank size)
Filter system
Filter cartridges (if required)
Air pump, airline, valve, check valve, airstone
Heater, thermometer
Electrical power strip with timer
Water treatment – dechlorinator
Fish net
Decorations: plastic plants, rocks, caves, ornaments
Siphon hose, algae brushes
Ammonia and pH test kits (or use the store's)
Other items such as ich medication and foods can wait until you
pick out your first fish on another trip.

Additional Equipment

There is a variety of equipment that can help with maintaining your animals in a healthy environment, or make aquarium cleaning tasks easier. Other than some form of aeration from an air pump (if sufficient aeration is not supplied by the filter), none of this equipment is mandatory for a basic freshwater aquarium. Automatic fish feeders may be helpful for people who are frequently away from home for a few days at a time. A battery-powered air pump (or even a gasoline generator) is vital for people who live in areas that experience frequent power outages.

Decorations

A wide variety of gravel, stones, plants, and other decorations are available for home aquariums. Not only do these items make the aquarium more attractive, they offer the fish places to hide and feel more secure. The most important aspect of any decorations is that they are safe for use inside aquariums. This means they must not contain toxic chemicals or metals that might corrode. Items purchased from a pet store will naturally be non-toxic, but people sometimes run into trouble when trying to use items they have around the house as decorations. A general rule of thumb is that if the material is considered safe for contact with human food, it should be safe for use in an aquarium.

Any decoration should be rinsed in tap water before placing it in an aquarium. Some items, such as driftwood and snail shells, may need to be soaked in water for a week or more to make certain there is no organic material still leaching from them. Of course, never use soap or detergents to clean anything that will later be placed inside an aquarium.

Live plants are popular with many fishkeepers trying to develop a more natural look for their aquariums. As mentioned, live plants require proper lighting in order to thrive. Some fish will feed on plants or uproot them from the gravel. There are some live

SMALL FRY

Diving Dogs and Pink Gravel!

While many home aquarium keepers strive to create a natural-looking environment for their fish, the fish themselves don't really care. A pirate skeleton that moves with air pressure from a pump will delight most youngsters. The shipwreck or castle ornaments have been favorites of some people for many years. Ceramic signs that say "No Fishing" or "Piranha Crossing" are considered high humor and are very popular. There really is no right or wrong way to approach aquarium design—the fish don't seem to mind as long as the materials used are non-toxic and they are given ample hiding spots.

Chloramines—Good for People, but Bad for Fish!

All municipal water supplies add disinfectants to the water to reduce bacteria levels, making the water safe for people to drink. One common chemical that is added is chlorine. In some cases, the city water supply also has methane gas in it. The chlorine then bonds with the methane to form trihalomethane, which has been known to cause cancer in humans. To keep that from happening, some cities add ammonia to the water to bond with the chlorine first, forming chloramines. These are safer for people, but more toxic to aquarium fish. If your city adds ammonia to its tap water, you need to neutralize the chloramines by first adding a double dose of aquarium dechlorinator. This breaks the tough chlorine/ammonia bond but leaves free ammonia. You should then add an ammonia-neutralizing compound to detoxify the ammonia. There are some one-step products on the market that will also take care of chloramines. Your local pet store can guide you to the correct product (since they no doubt have to use the products themselves for their own aquariums!).

plants such as "princess pines" that will stay green in an aquarium for a few months but not grow. Sometimes, houseplants such as the peace lily are sold as aquarium plants; these also will not grow well. One simple test is to hold the aquarium plant by its base out of the water. If it flops over, it is definitely a true aquatic plant. The leaves of terrestrial plants will remain upright. One exception to this is the different types of *Anubias* plant. These will remain standing upright when lifted out of the water, but they are true aquatic plants and actually do very well.

The five top aquarium plants for beginners include *Anubias*, *Cryptocoryne,* Java fern, Java moss, and water sprite.

Step-by-Step Installation Instructions

The following steps are generalized instructions for setting up a typical small- to medium-sized home aquarium. If your dealer or the products themselves give different instructions, those should be followed instead.

1. Go to the store and buy all the equipment you'll need (see checklist).

2. Install the background on the back of the aquarium.

3. Determine the location for the stand, then place the empty tank on the stand and make sure it is level.

4. Rinse the gravel (a small amount at a time) in a bucket with tap water until it runs clear.

5. Install the undergravel filter plate (if used) and then add the rinsed gravel to the tank, sloping it gently from lower in the front to higher in the back.

6. Using tap water that is between 60° and 80°, fill the tank one

quarter full and re-check that the tank is still level. It helps to use your hand or a small plate to keep the water from disturbing the gravel bed.

7. Fill the tank 90 percent full and check the level again. Look for any tank leaks (although this is very rare nowadays, tanks used to leak fairly often). Fill the tank the rest of the way. Usually this is about 1 inch (2.5 cm) from the top, but this depends on the type of aquarium.

8. Install the heater and thermometer, but do not plug the heater in. Add any decorations.

9. Install the hang-on-back filter (if used) and connect the airline to the valves and the air pump. Leave a drip loop on every electrical cord that is attached to a device in your tank. That way, if water should ever travel down the cord, it will drip off rather than follow the cord all the way to the electrical outlet.

10. Plug the heater in and check the water temperature on the thermometer. Turn the heater dial down (usually counterclockwise) until the heater's pilot light just goes out. The heater is now set to hold whatever temperature the water is at that point. Adjust the temperature up or down as needed by turning the heater adjustment knob a quarter turn at a time. When the light goes out, the heater is now maintaining that new temperature. Check the thermometer to see what it is, and repeat the process as needed. Some heaters have built-in temperatures on their dials. These should only be used as estimates; use your thermometer to read the actual water temperature.

11. Add water dechlorinator or other recommended pre-treatment. Place the hood on the tank, making any necessary cutouts so the top fits around the filter. Turn the lights on.

12. Wait 24 hours and check the water temperature, and adjust again if needed. If the water is clear and all the equipment is operating properly, you can now go back to the pet store to buy your first few hardy fish and begin cycling the tank!

When filling an aquarium, you can use a plate or bowl to prevent water from disturbing the gravel bed.

Chapter 3

First Inhabitants:

Hardy Fish Choices

This chapter describes a number of hardy, inexpensive, yet desirable species of fish that make good choices for beginning home aquarium keepers. You should read this section and look at the pictures to get a general idea of the fish you may want to buy. After that, you should read Chapter 5, which describes the process of buying your first fish.

The majority of home aquariums are relatively small, tropical freshwater tanks. Beginning aquarists almost always select this type of tank to start out with. The fish in this section are all hardy, colorful, and smaller varieties that have a good track record of thriving in tanks such as these. Fish can jump out or come down with diseases, but for the most part, by selecting your aquarium inhabitants from the fish listed in this chapter, you will be more successful. Later on, as you gain more experience, you may decide to try intermediate and advanced aquariums outlined in chapters six and seven.

Angelfish

A peaceful member of the cichlid family, angelfish (*Pterophyllum scalare*), have been popular with home aquarists for many years. Originally coming from South America, different varieties have been developed. Some have lacey fins, others have different color patterns, but all can grow to around 4 inches (10 cm) tall. Angelfish feed readily on flakes and small pellets, as well as brine shrimp and live foods. Because they spend much of their time hovering, they do not require as much space as more active swimmers. They may nip at the fins of other fish and will try to eat small juvenile fish of other species. In recent years, the young of the fancier types have proven to be more delicate. This may be due to inbreeding or some unknown disease.

Barbs

Very hardy and active, barbs are members of the minnow family. Some, such as the tinfoil barb, grow very large, while others, such as the tiger barb, can be aggressive toward smaller fish or may nip at the fins of larger, slower fish. Gold and cherry barbs are two species that stay small and are peaceful and colorful. Barbs feed well on flakes or small pellets and will take food from the surface and even the tank bottom. Most species do best in schools of five or more fish.

Bettas

Also known as the Siamese fighting fish, bettas (*Betta splendens*) grow to

Angelfish spend most of their time hovering and do not require as much room as a more active swimmer.

SMALL FRY

Dear Diary

Keeping a diary of your aquariums (often called a log book) can be an important way to keep information (data) about your animals. Information you will want to keep about the animals can include; the date you got a fish, what its favorite food is, fish that it gets along with, you can even add a picture or drawing of the fish. You should also keep information about the aquarium itself, such as; water temperature, date of the last water change, when you added new decorations, or any other notable event. This information can be useful later on, even years later, by telling you how long a fish lived, or how long an aquarium was set up.

resist nipping at the betta's long flowing fins. Because bettas can utilize oxygen directly from the air, they do not require aeration or even filtration systems. Many people elect to keep them in a small container by themselves, but remember that they are a tropical species and do not fare well at normal room temperature. These fish prefer to feed on natural food items such as bloodworms or brine shrimp. They do not usually accept flake foods, but there are new "betta pellets" on the market that are accepted well and very convenient to use. There was a fad for trying to keep a betta in a vase with a peace lily plant growing out of it. These were supposed to never need feeding or water changes. Of course, the fish would only survive a few months under such conditions, so the fad has mostly died out (along with the fish subjected to this poor care!).

43

2.5 inches (6.5 cm) long, not including the long flowing caudal fin. They were originally found in Southeast Asia, but all of the bettas sold in pet stores have been captive raised for enhanced colors and longer fins. These fish can be problematic if not cared for properly. Two male bettas will fight each other for territory, and some other fish cannot

Bettas need to be kept at tropical temperatures, but they do not require aeration or filtration systems.

Hardy Fish Choices

Gouramis

Gouramis are medium- to large-sized fish found mostly in Southeast Asia. Like bettas, they are labyrinth fishes, which have a lung-like organ and can breathe air from the surface. Gouramis have elongated pelvic fins, like threads that they use to feel along the bottom in cloudy waters where they live in the wild. The paradise fish (*Macropodus opercularis*) has very similar habits except that they can tolerate subtropical temperatures. In most species, the males are more colorful than the females.

Cory Catfish

Cory catfish (*Corydoras* spp.) hail from tropical rivers and streams of South America. They grow to a maximum size of only 2.5 inches (6.4 cm) and prefer a water temperature of around 78°F (26°C). Feeding is not a problem, as cory catfish readily accept a variety of sinking meat-based flakes and pellets. If there are other, more active fish in the aquarium, you need to make sure that some food gets to the bottom where these catfish prefer to feed. Cory cats have two unique behaviors; they will periodically rush to the surface and take a breath of air, and they sometimes roll their eyeballs downward, making it look like they are blinking at you. If you buy a cory cat, expect it to be around for quite a while, as they are hardy and have been known to live over ten years in captivity. Some cory catfish are still caught in the wild, and these tend to be less hardy than captive-raised ones.

Suckermouth Catfish

Suckermouth cats are armored catfish found in Central and South America. The most commonly seen species is the plecostomus (*Hypostomus plecostomus*). However, these tend to grow too large for many home

Cory catfish are hardy charges that can live for more than ten years in captivity.

A Note About Collection Planning

The very first fish you select for your aquarium will set the tone for that tank in regard to every other fish you want to add later on. Make this choice carefully so you aren't forced to pass by more desirable fish in the future just because they are not compatible. Chapter four outlines the best process to follow in getting your first fish.

Giant danios reach large sizes and require a 50-gallon aquarium at minimum.

aquariums, reaching a length of 19 inches (50 cm). There are many smaller species that do better in home aquariums, such as the bristlenose (*Ancistrus* spp.) and *Otocinclus*. Many suckermouth catfish feed on algae, and one good way to feed them is by means of algae wafer, a sinking flat disk of food that they are especially fond of. Most of these fish also enjoy rasping away at driftwood to feed on the algae growing on it.

Danios

These very active minnows are found throughout Asia and India. Danios require more room for their size than most other aquarium fish. They are very hardy, feed readily on flake foods, and are peaceful toward other fish. You can tell by their upturned mouths that danios are adapted to feeding from the water's surface. For small aquariums, the zebra danio (*Danio rerio*) is a good choice, as it only reaches 1.5 inches (3.8 cm) in length. Zebra danios are available in a variety of color patterns and fin types. There is even a genetically modified version (see chapter six). The white cloud (*Tanichthys albonubes*) is similar to the zebra danio in its habits. Found in China and Vietnam, it is a subtropical species that can survive in temperatures as low as 50°F (10°C). The giant danio (*Devario malabaricus*) reaches 4.5 inches (12 cm) and a school of these may require a 50-gallon (190-liter) or larger aquarium to truly be comfortable.

Goldfish

For as popular as they have been for hundreds of years, goldfish (*Carassius auratus*) are not always the best choices for home aquariums containing mixed groups of fish. Goldfish prefer cooler water than tropical species, and they grow quite large, capable of reaching a length of 10 inches (25 cm). Avoid the common goldfish that are sold as "feeder fish" for large carnivorous fish. These feeder goldfish are very inexpensive, but they are not handled well by the dealers and often die within a week or two. If you want to keep goldfish, consider setting up a larger, unheated aquarium and focus on just this species. There are so many color varieties and forms of goldfish that it can almost be like having a mixed species tank anyway!

Guppies

The guppy (*Poecilia reticulata*) is likely the second most popular aquarium fish (after the goldfish). A livebearing species, people have developed many strains over the years that have different color and fin structure. Originally from the Caribbean and South America, the guppy has been introduced throughout the world as a hoped-for means to control mosquitoes. The guppy feeds well on crumbled flake foods and prefers to feed from the surface. Males tend to chase the females, so it often helps to have more females than males in the tank so no single female gets picked on too much. Male fancy guppies, with their long flowing caudal fins, are sometimes a target for nippy fish such as barbs. The closely related Endler's livebearer (*Poecilia wingei*) has become very popular in recent years.

Platies

Platies (*Xiphophorus maculatus* and *X. variatus*) are related livebearers that stay relatively small, are peaceful, and come in a variety of colors. They

Fancy Platies

Platies, like other fancy livebearers, come in a wide array of colors, body shapes, and fin shapes. Here are just a few you might find.

Balloon: rounded belly, shortened body length

Hi-fin: taller-than-normal dorsal fin

Lyretail: elongated upper and lower extensions on the tail fin

Sail-fin: elongated dorsal fin, often fanlike

Bleeding heart: red spots at center of body

Mickey Mouse: has an arrangement of three spots on the tail that resembles the famous mouse

Painted: mixed black spots on a red or orange body

Sunset: dark orange or red tail

Tuxedo: black stripe running down the center of the body

Velvet: bright solid color, usually red

Wagtail: black caudal fin

Male swordtails feature a long extension on the lower edge of their tail fin.

rarely grow larger than 2 inches (5 cm) and do well in most home aquariums. The common names for each variety describe the different colors and fin types, many of which can be found in different combinations.

Mollies are a related type of livebearer, but as pointed out in chapter five, they have slightly more specialized requirements.

Swordtails

Another member of the livebearer group, it is the long extension on the lower edge of the tail fin of the male fish that gives the swordtail (*Xiphophorus hellerii*) its common name. They have been developed into a number of color varieties and fin shapes that correlates with the names given in the sidebar on platies. Swordtails do grow larger than other livebearers (except for sail-fin mollies). Few fish can compare to the brilliant color of a red velvet swordtail.

Loaches

Loaches are active, bottom-dwelling fish found throughout Asia. Most species have tiny whiskers as well as spines on their cheeks. The kuhli (sometimes spelled coolie) loach (*Pangio kuhlii*) is one of the more popular species. The colorful clown loach (*Chromobotia macracanthus*) is also very popular but more expensive. Loaches tend to leave other fish alone and therefore make good tankmates for a wide variety of fish species. One drawback to keeping loaches is their sensitivity to certain ich medications, making it difficult to treat them should they come down with this disease. If caught early enough, raising the water temperature a few degrees and using the ich medication at half the normal dose will cure a sick loach.

Rainbowfish

Rainbowfish are active, colorful tropical fish that come from northern Australia, through New Guinea and into the Southeast Asian islands. The most

Mature rainbowfish generally display vivid coloration.

common genus in the aquarium trade is *Melanotaenia*, which is Greek for "black-banded," referring to the banding some of these fish possess. They do best if kept in groups of five or more, as they prefer to swim in schools. Feeding is no problem, as they will accept most types of flake foods right from the surface. Young rainbowfish of all species tend to be pale in color, as do rainbowfish kept over light-colored gravel. The mature males show the most vibrant colors.

Rasboras

These small members of the minor family hail from Southeast Asia west through Africa. While closely related to danios, rasboras are a bit more peaceful and delicate like small tetras. The harlequin rasbora (*Trigonostigma heteromorpha*) is one of the most popular species. While these fish will

eat flake food, they do much better if also fed planktonic foods such as brine shrimp or daphnia. Recently, some very small but brightly colored rasboras and related species have become available in pet stores. These diminutive fish do well in nano aquariums, with live plants, and no aggressive fish.

Sharks

Whoever decided to name these minnows "sharks" should get some sort of marketing award. Many people buy these for their aquarium based solely on their notorious name (although they are interesting fish in their own right). The red-tailed black shark (*Epalzeorhynchos bicolor*) is perhaps the most attractive member of the group, with a bright red tail and dark charcoal black body. It is the triangular dorsal fin of these fish that reminds people of a true shark. The

Five Great Starter Fish

1. Bloodfin tetra
2. Cherry barb
3. Cory catfish
4. Red wag platy
5. White cloud

key to keeping these sharks is to only add one to the tank (they fight with one another and with related species) and to keep the aquarium tightly covered, as they are excellent jumpers. These fish spend much of their time swimming along the bottom or up the sides of the aquarium. They feed well on flake food or small plankton that is allowed to settle on the bottom. Some "sharks" such as the iridescent shark, grow much too large for any home aquarium. Other species, such as the rainbow shark, may outgrow all but the largest home aquariums. Always look up the adult size of the fish before you purchase it.

There are two species of shark to always avoid, the iridescent shark and the Colombian (or black-fin) shark. Both are actually species of catfish that can grow to over 3 feet (91 cm) long!

Tetras

Tetras are small fish from South America (although a few species are found in Africa). You can tell a tetra from many other species of fish because they have a tiny, fleshy adipose fin along their back, behind their dorsal fin, but in front of the tail. There are a huge number of tetra species, including the infamous piranha and the giant pacu. Beginning home aquarists are better off choosing a small colorful tetra such as the bloodfin or lemon. The small tetras are all peaceful, schooling fish that do best when added to aquariums with live plants that have been set up for a few months. Crumbled flake food serves as a good food for most species.

The red-tailed black shark, like all freshwater sharks, must be the only member of its species in a given tank, as they are known to be aggressive and territorial with their own kind.

Chapter 4

Ready, Set, Go!

Getting Your First Fish

So, here you are halfway through the book, and you are just now going to learn how to get your first fish! The information in this chapter is vital. It never pays to just rush out and buy some fish; you need to develop a strategy first.

Planning Your Collection

As mentioned in chapter three, the very first fish you buy for your aquarium sets the overall tone for your tank and determines what other types of fish you will be able to add later on. Some fish are peaceful and many other species will get along with them, while a few fish are so aggressive that they can't be kept with any other fish. Some fish have specific water quality requirements that other fish do not share—you would have difficulty keeping brackish water mollies with soft water tetras, for example. Do you want to see shoals of small fish drifting peacefully through aquatic plants? If so, you need to remember that big fish often eat little fish, so you won't be able to keep an African cichlid in that same tank.

It will help to go through chapter three to get some basic ideas of what fish interest you. You should also visit your local pet store to see what type of fishes they have in stock (although this will change from week to week). Make a list of the species you are interested in and select one or two types to start with.

How Many Fish of What Size?

A very common question asked by beginning home aquarists is how many fish a tank can hold. This is called the stocking rate. This rate takes into account the type of fish being considered, the swimming needs of the fish, as well as the number of fish and their potential adult size. Aquariums can be overcrowded in three ways. There is a biological limit where there simply are not enough beneficial bacteria present to detoxify the amount of fish waste being produced. If the biological limit is exceeded, the ammonia and nitrite levels will rise, poisoning the fish. Aquariums also have a territorial

If you choose to keep a school of small, peaceful fish, you cannot add a large, aggressive one to the tank later on.

limit where the addition of certain other fish will cause serious fighting among the inhabitants. Finally, there is a swimming room limit. An aquarium must have enough room for the fish to swim around and exhibit normal behaviors.

Biological Limit

There have been many attempts to answer the basic question of how many fish a tank can hold, but most of them are flawed. You see, they usually give this stocking rate as "so many inches of fish per gallon of water." This actually compares two unrelated units of measure, length and volume, so it can't work. It would be like saying that a car gets 100 pounds to the mile. As a fish's length increases linearly (from 1 to 2 inches, for example) the volume goes up by the cube, changing the ratio. The example that makes this clearer is that while you might be able to keep twenty 1-inch tetras in a 24-inch-long, 15-gallon aquarium, just try putting one 20-inch pacu in the same tank—all of the water would splash out! Even though the "inches of fish" were the same at 20 inches total, the single 20-inch fish weighs about 70 times more than the 20 smaller fish combined!

Another factor that needs to be considered is the effectiveness of the filtration system used. An aquarium with an efficient filter will have a higher biological limit than a tank with a small economy filter. Finally, the water exchange rate affects the aquarium's ability to properly house

Let's Go to the Fish Store

One of my favorite memories as a young child was taking a trip to a nearby town with my father on weekends to buy new fish for our home aquarium. I would save up my allowance, and we would drive about an hour to get to the pet store. This particular store had types of fish that I had never seen before at our neighborhood pet store. I would then look at all the fish and decide which one I could afford. The problem was that we did not research the species of fish before I bought them, and we didn't ask the pet store worker enough questions. We often ended up bringing home fish that did not thrive in our particular aquarium. You can make your own even better memories if you research new fish before you buy them.

fish. A tank that gets a 25 percent water change each and every week is going to be able to house more fish than an aquarium that only gets a water change once every month or two.

So what method can you use to determine the number of fish that an aquarium can house? Fisheries biologists often use the weight of the fish per gallon of water (since fish weigh as much as the water they displace, it is the same as comparing volume to volume). For a normal home aquarium, a normal value for this is around 1 gram of fish weight per gallon of water (0.27 grams per liter). Crowded conditions would be seen at a rate of 1.5 to 2 grams per gallon (up to 0.54 grams per liter). Obviously, you cannot easily weigh your home aquarium fish. The best that can be done is to see examples in the sidebar that have been shown to work, and then try to duplicate them. Remember that unless you buy them as adults, your fish will grow and require more room as they get older.

Swimming Room for Fish

Swimming room is also an important factor for most fish—they need to have room to swim, turn, and interact with each other. Many of the calculations that have been used have the same flaw as mentioned before: stating that a 4-inch fish requires 30 gallons of swimming space, for example. Again, this is comparing a fish's length to water volume, and it cannot work. What works better is to measure the open water length and width of your aquarium and add them together. This gives a linear measure. The height of an aquarium is usually proportional to its

Different Stocking Amounts for a 20-gallon (76-liter) Tank

Thirty	1-inch (2.5-cm)	tetras
Fifteen	1.5-inch (3.8-cm)	rasboras
Eight	2-inch (5-cm)	livebearer fish or barbs
Four	3-inch (7.6-cm)	angelfish
One	6-inch (12.7-cm)	cichlid

Body Style 1 Minimum ratio 1:4	Body Style 2 Minimum ratio 1:7	Body Style 3 Minimum ratio 1:9
Bettas	Barbs	Danios
Corydoras catfish	Cichlids (most)	Kuhli loach (divide length by 2)
Eels (divide length by 3)	Cyprinids – minnows	Monos
Gobies	Goldfish	Pangasiid shark-catfish
Killifish	Gouramis	Pictus catfish
Plecostomus	Poeciliids – livebearers	Rainbowfish
Puffer fish	Rasboras	Sailfin mollies
Suckermouth catfish	Tetras	Silversides (Atherinids)

length, so you don't need to be concerned with that measurement. Next, determine the adult captive size that the fish is expected to grow to.

You can either get this data from aquarium books or estimate it by looking up the fish on www.fishbase. org. The final step is to make a ratio of the fish's length to open water swimming room. If the fish has a maximum adult size of 4 inches and your tank measures 30 inches long and 12 inches wide, the ratio would be 4:42. You need to reduce this so the first number is a one. To do this, divide the second number by the first number (42 divided by 4 = 10.5). Your working ratio is then 1:10.5. These ratios work the same whether you are using English measurements, as in this example, or metric units. Just be consistent with which you use.

Armed with that information, you then determine which of the three categories your fish belongs to. If

you are in doubt, select category two as a compromise. The final step is to compare the ratio you calculated to the minimum ratios given. Make sure that none of the fish you want to buy will fall below the minimum ratio. You do not need to calculate this ratio for every single fish in your aquarium, just the one that has the potential to grow the longest.

Compatibility

Determining which fish will coexist peacefully in an aquarium is more of an art than a science. The basic compatibility chart is a useful starting point in selecting compatible fish. Understand though, that in the end, fish are individuals and not always going to follow any set of rules. Even fish that have lived together peacefully for years can suddenly begin fighting. It is always best to have a backup plan for what you can do should your fish stop getting along. If you have

Kuhli loaches have elongated body shapes and would seem to need more horizontal swimming space than many other fish. They are bottom dwellers however, so only need as much room as a normal fish half their length.

multiple aquariums, you may have enough options to move your fish around as needed. If you have just one tank, you may want to invest in a tank divider. These plastic perforated plates are used to keep incompatible fish separated in an aquarium while still allowing water to flow from one end of the tank to the other.

Selecting Individual Fish

Now comes the time for you to visit your local pet store and buy your first fish. You may want to confirm your fish stocking plan with store employees and gain their approval. While this book gives you good general information, the pet store employees can offer you specifics about the fish they have in stock.

In choosing an individual fish, you should look at all of the fish in the tank to ensure they are healthy. One sick fish can very easily infect all of the others because fish diseases transmit so easily through the water. Look especially

closely for signs that the fish might have ich (see chapter five). The fish should be actively swimming, without ripped fins or other wounds, and their eyes should be clear. The tank should be clean, and the water should be clear, not cloudy.

When it comes to selecting what individual fish you want to buy, remember that the pet store employee may have difficulty in capturing a specific fish from a tank full of identical species. The general rule is that if there are big differences in the fish (differently colored fancy guppies, for example), or if there are less than six fish in the tank, you should feel comfortable pointing out exactly which fish you want. For tanks filled with similar fish, it is usually best to first observe them to make sure there are no damaged fish in the tank, and then let the employee pick the fish out. Remember, though, that the fish most easily caught may also have some problem that made it slower than its

Basic Aquarium Fish Compatibility Chart

	Angelfish	Barb	Betta	Cory	Danio	Goldfish	Gourami	Livebearer	Loach	Rainbowfish	Rasbora	Shark	Tetra
Angelfish	Yes	May	May	Yes	Yes	May	Yes	Yes	Yes	Yes	Yes	Yes	Yes
Barbs	May	Yes	No	Yes	Yes	Yes	Yes	Yes	Yes	Yes	May	Yes	Yes
Bettas	May	No	No	Yes	No	No	No	May	Yes	No	May	No	May
Cory cat	Yes	Yes	Yes	Yes	Yes	Yes	Yes	Yes	Yes	Yes	Yes	Yes	Yes
Danio	Yes	Yes	No	Yes	Yes	Yes	Yes	May	Yes	Yes	May	Yes	May
Goldfish	May	Yes	No	Yes	Yes	Yes	Yes	May	Yes	Yes	No	May	No
Gourami	Yes	Yes	No	Yes	Yes	Yes	Yes	Yes	Yes	Yes	May	Yes	May
Livebearer	Yes	Yes	May	Yes	May	May	Yes	Yes	Yes	Yes	Yes	Yes	Yes
Loach	Yes	Yes	Yes	Yes	Yes	Yes	Yes	Yes	Yes	Yes	Yes	Yes	Yes
Rainbowfish	Yes	Yes	No	Yes	Yes	Yes	Yes	Yes	Yes	Yes	May	Yes	May
Rasbora	Yes	May	May	Yes	May	No	May	Yes	Yes	May	Yes	May	Yes
Shark	Yes	Yes	No	Yes	Yes	May	Yes	Yes	Yes	Yes	May	No	May
Tetra	Yes	Yes	May	Yes	May	No	May	Yes	Yes	May	Yes	May	Yes

To use this chart, read where a row and column intersect. The cell content describes the expected compatibility of two species of fish. This assumes that the fish in question are the normal size sold in pet stores. "No" means there is very little chance those two species will get along together. "Yes" means they will coexist in most instances. "May" indicates there may be members of the group that won't get along or that individual fish behavior will influence their compatibility so it cannot be easily predicted.

Healthy fish have clear eyes and no visible wounds or ripped fins.

such cases, you may want to ask for a different specimen.

Acclimation

Whenever a fish is moved from one aquarium to another, it undergoes some degree of stress. If the difference in temperature or pH between the water in the two tanks is great enough, the fish could die from shock. Acclimation is the process of allowing a fish to gradually adjust from one water type to another.

Your new fish will typically be placed in small plastic bags at the pet store. Usually, a third of the bag is filled with water and the rest with either air or oxygen. Then the top is tied in a knot or sealed with a rubber band. If the store uses air to fill the bag, you should plan on getting your fish home within 30 minutes or so. If the store uses pure oxygen, the fish can remain in their bags

tankmates! Watch how the employee catches the fish—did they have to chase the fish all around the tank? Did it take them a long time to make the capture? Did the net come up with lots of gravel in it as well as the fish? Did the fish flop out of the net and onto the floor? All of these things show that the capture did not go well, and the fish may have been severely stressed. In

To Catch a Fish!

Catching a fish in an aquarium can be difficult. It takes lots of practice to become good at it. Some fish are more difficult to capture than others. Never chase a fish with the net—they can always swim faster than you can push the net through the water! Try using two nets and herd the fish into one net with the other. Never pin the net against the side of the tank—the fish could get pinched. Fish get wise very quickly; if you don't manage to capture the fish in the first minute or so, stop and try again later. One trick that may work is to sprinkle a little fish food on the surface while holding the net above the tank. As the fish rise to feed, you may be able to scoop down with the net and capture them. If you are out of town a lot, you may want to invest in an electronic feeder that will place a set amount of food into the tank every day for you.

much longer, even over 24 hours. During transport to your home, the fish need to be kept in the dark and at the proper temperature. Once you arrive home, the physical acclimation process can begin. If your pet store supplies you with instructions on how they

Drip acclimation container with an airline and knotted water inflow line. Drip acclimation is one way to gradually allow fish to adjust from one water type to another.

want you to acclimate their fish, you may want to follow them. Otherwise, proceed as follows:

1. Turn off the aquarium lights and float the bag at the surface of the tank. After about 15 minutes, the water temperature in the bag will be the same as the water in the tank.

2. Open the bag and carefully pour about half of the water into a container. Take care that the fish doesn't slide out during this process!

3. Next, turn the top of the plastic bag down and in on itself a few times to form a floatation collar. You may find that the bag is less likely to tip over if you use a clip like a clothespin to attach it to the side of the tank.

4. Add some water from the tank to the bag. This amount should be approximately 25 percent of the

volume of water that was in the bag at step 3. Wait five minutes.

5. Remove some water from the bag by pouring it into a container (not back into the tank). Add water from the tank to the bag again, but this time, add double the amount of water you added in step 4. Wait another five minutes.

6. Repeat step 5. This gives a total acclimation time of 30 minutes, which is appropriate for all basic freshwater fish purchased at a local pet store. Fish that have been shipped to you by overnight express will require a different acclimation procedure. Check with your dealer for instructions.

7. Gently release the fish into the aquarium.

Watch all the fish in the aquarium closely for the first day. Try feeding them to see if the new fish are feeding properly. Watch for fighting between

When acclimating fish, float a bag in an aquarium to equalize the water temperature in the bag and the water temperature in the tank.

the old and new fish. Some chasing almost always occurs, but if any of the fish develop ripped and torn fins, they may need to be isolated.

Quarantine

There is always a danger that a new fish will bring some disease into your tank and infect all of your fish. You can minimize this problem by choosing your fish carefully, but the risk never entirely goes away. Public aquariums and people who have very expensive fish collections (like some marine aquarists have) will quarantine all new fish to reduce this risk even further. This process isolates any new fish for a time so any diseases they may be carrying can be identified and treated. To do this, you'll need a

Beware of Anything That Doesn't Look Right!

If you see something about your aquarium or fish that seems unusual, it is vital that you stop and take a moment to investigate why. Too many times, people ignore a minor first symptom and are then faced with a larger problem later on. There is always an underlying reason for a change in a fish's behavior. One example is a group of Oscar cichlids I noticed one morning, lined up next to one another facing the front of the aquarium, but resting on the bottom. That definitely didn't look right, but because the fish looked so comical doing that, it wasn't thought to be serious. A day later, white spots appeared on the fish. They had contracted ich and had to be treated. While they all survived, it was a close call, and any further delay would have resulted in some of the fish dying.

What to Do with an Unwanted Fish?

Despite your best intentions, there may come a time when you need to close down your aquarium and find a new home for your fish. Your first choice should be to see if friends or family can take the fish. If that doesn't work, you can try contacting the pet store where you purchased them. If the fish are healthy, your local pet store may be able take them back and find new homes for them.

Under no circumstances should you ever release a pet fish into the wild! This apparent kindness can have only two outcomes; the fish dies or is eaten by another animal, or it thrives and potentially becomes an invasive species. It is actually against the law to release an aquarium fish into any natural waters in the United States.

If you have a seriously sick fish, or one you simply cannot find a home for, you may need to consider euthanizing it. This is more humane (and better for the environment) than releasing it into the wild. If you need to do this, the basic method is to place the fish in a bowl of its water, with a snap on lid. Place this in the freezer for 24 hours. Since the fish is used to tropical temperatures, it will gradually just slow down as the water gets colder. Once the water freezes solid, the now unconscious fish will simply die. While this process may seem harsh, it is really for the best.

Remember that pet ownership comes with some very serious responsibilities!

dedicated quarantine tank, and this is sometimes too costly for beginning home aquarists to manage. Still, having a quarantine tank can be helpful, not only when buying new fish, but for isolating any of your existing fish for one reason or another.

Observing Your Fish

Watching your fish is really why you have an aquarium in the first place — you cannot enjoy your tank if you don't look at it! Proper observation can also show you impending disease problems, or if some fish are not getting along together. Fish are quite able to see outside their aquarium—they soon learn to beg at the water's surface for food when they see you enter the room. Because fish will interact with movement outside their tank (and this changes their behavior), it is best to make your observations from a darkened room and the aquarium light on. Fish cannot see you under these conditions, so their behavior will not include reacting to your presence. It is important to observe your fish every day, not just at feeding time.

Chapter 5

Maintaining Your Aquarium

The fun doesn't stop after you add fish to the aquarium. This section describes how to best maintain your home aquarium, keeping the fish healthy and the life support system operating flawlessly.

Feeding and Nutrition

Proper nutrition is vital to all animals. The fish in your aquarium rely solely on you to supply all of their dietary needs. Your fish's diet must be of sufficient quantity to supply the energy the fish needs to grow. The diet must also have the proper balance of fats, proteins, and carbohydrates. The food also needs to have the proper amount of vitamins and minerals. Too much food or food too high in calories will cause the fish to become obese. Not all fish have the same dietary requirements, and these needs even change as a fish grows. To top it off, overfeeding an aquarium can result in deteriorating water quality that will harm the fish.

Luckily, there are many good fish foods on the market, and most of the fish suitable for your freshwater aquarium will have similar dietary requirements. The basic dietary needs of each fish species are given in chapter three, and your pet store can help direct you to what specific brand of food will work well for you. Most beginning home aquarium keepers choose to feed their fish a variety of flake food or small pelleted foods. You may want to avoid buying the "jumbo economy size" fish foods—because you have a small freshwater aquarium, the food may become stale or crumble to dust before you reach the bottom of the canister, and you won't really save any money because that food will have been wasted.

Once you have selected the types of food you'll be feeding your fish, the feeding frequency and amount are the next things to consider. Most small fish such as neon tetras do best if fed twice a day (some baby fish may need to be fed four or more times per day). Medium-sized fish like gouramis or danios should be fed once a day. Some very large fish may only need to be fed three times per week.

The amount of food you feed is very important, and you can let your fish tell you how much to feed them! The basic process is to place a very small amount of food in the tank and let the fish eat all of it up. If the food is settling to the bottom in large amounts, you are either feeding too much food or adding it too quickly. Once the fish have finished their original amount of food, add a bit more and let them eat all of that. Continue this process for two to four minutes and then stop, even if the fish are

There is a wide range of prepared fish foods on the market.

SMALL FRY

Hand Feeding Your Fish

Something fun to try is to train your fish to take bits of food from your hand. Most fish will soon recognize that you usually feed them when you lift the aquarium's lid. It takes just a little effort to then get the fish to feed from your fingers. Some fish are better students than others. Bottom-dwelling catfish and small schooling fish will rarely learn to hand feed. Gouramis, bettas, cichlids, and other large fish usually learn very quickly.

The first thing is to get the fish accustomed to your presence at feeding time. This can take a few weeks to a month. Once they wriggle their bodies in anticipation of your approach, you begin gradually moving your hand closer to the water's surface each day. If the fish shy away, you are taking the process too fast.

Eventually, you will be able to submerge your fingertips in the water while the fish are feeding around them (make certain that you rinse your hands well before this step, as soap residue can harm the fish).

The final step is to pinch a bit of food between your fingers and submerge them slowly and hold very still. The fish will come up and take the food right from your hand. Eventually, you may be able to lead the fish around the tank with your hand as they chase after the food.

still begging for food. What will happen is that in the next feeding, the fish will be left a little hungry from the first and eat their food faster. Since you are feeding them on demand, you will end up adding more food during that same time frame and they will get enough to eat. Likewise, if you feed too much food, the fish will feed at a slower rate at the next feeding and you will end up giving them less food.

This method works well for feeding flake foods to all fish except for bottom feeders such as catfish. You need to make sure that a little of the food sinks to the bottom where the catfish can find it. Remember that almost every new aquarium keeper (especially children!) tend to overfeed their fish—having a fish actually starve in an aquarium is very rare. Overfeeding will cause fouled water that will quickly kill the fish in a newly set-up aquarium.

Disease Control

Despite your best efforts, your fish will likely become sick at some point. This happens to virtually everyone; even professional public aquarists need to be able to deal with sick fish. The first defense against disease is to observe your fish carefully, at least once a day, for possible signs of problems. Catching problems early on is vital. If the very first observation you make that something is wrong is that one or more of your fish has died, you probably will not be able to act quickly enough to save the remaining fish. For some problems such as tumors, there is really nothing that you as a home aquarist can do for the fish, and ineffective treatments can cause more harm than good. The following section identifies the common fish ailments and indicates a proper treatment (if any) for them.

Accidental Poisoning

Many chemicals can be dissolved in aquarium water, and some of these are toxic to fish. There have been cases where aquarium fish were poisoned due to air in the room being contaminated or something placed into the aquarium that allowed chemicals to be released. Poisoning, because it is usually invisible, is sometimes unfairly blamed for fish deaths where there seems to be no other possible reason than "an unknown poison." In many of these cases, there were explainable reasons for the fish loss (like a disease) but the aquarist just missed the symptoms.

Gases in the room where the aquarium is located account for many instances of accidental poisoning. Cigarette smoke, disinfectants, and room air-fresheners usually only cause problems at very high concentrations. However, insecticides and paint fumes can be much more dangerous. Beware of pest control applicators and painting contractors who tell you that all you need to do is unplug your tank's air pump and drape it with plastic and the fish will

be safe—they may not be. A good rule of thumb is if the room's air quality is bothersome to humans, it will be harmful to the fish.

The next most common form of poisoning is through direct contact. A person may have some strong detergent residue on their hands, and these dissolve into the water when the person reaches into the tank. Small children may place things in the aquarium (pennies can be very toxic due to their copper and zinc content). The aquarist may add a decoration that isn't safe (nontoxic choices are outlined in chapter two). These types of direct poisoning are linked to the aquarium's volume. A small bit of soap residue may not be an issue in a large aquarium, but the same amount in a small tank could be a problem. One general rule of thumb is if the

Observe your fish carefully every day to make sure nothing is wrong.

Make sure any decorations are safe for fish before adding them to an aquarium.

material is safe for direct contact with human food, it will be safe for your aquarium fish as well.

Another method by which aquarium water can be poisoned is through something added deliberately by the aquarist for a particular reason. Maybe you added a chemical with instructions to add a teaspoon, and you misread it and added a tablespoon. Some antibiotics used to treat bacterial diseases in fish can disrupt the biological filter system, causing a rise in ammonia and nitrite levels (as explained in chapter one). Anti-protozoan medications that contain malachite green may prove toxic to delicate fish, and even hardy fish can be killed if the tank is not dosed correctly.

If you are certain that there is a case of poisoning in your aquarium, and the fish look like they are in a bad way, your best course of action

will be to draw some water from the tap at the same temperature as the aquarium, add dechlorinator, wait a couple of minutes, and move the fish directly to a new container. Never mind about acclimating the fish; they need to get out of the poisoned water as soon as possible. After the fish are safe, you can then decide how to remove the contaminants from the aquarium (usually by draining all of the water and rinsing everything well with tap water).

Anchorworms, Copepods (*Lernaea*)

Despite their common name, anchorworms are copepod crustaceans, not worms. Their name comes from the first symptom that aquarium keepers see—twin wormlike egg sacs of the female copepod emerging from the fish's skin like a "V." What you cannot see are the parasitic males and females that don't yet have egg sacs that are also living on the fish's skin.

This disease usually comes into an aquarium from fish that were raised in outdoor ponds. It can be very difficult to eradicate because any poisons strong enough to kill this hard-shelled parasite may also harm the fish in the tank. Some people advocate removing the egg sacs with a pair of forceps—this will help reduce the number of parasites, but it will not eliminate them. One treatment that works for fish that can tolerate some salt in their water is to raise the salt content to 0.75 percent for 21 days. To do this, add 10 grams of synthetic sea salt per gallon of aquarium water every other day for three additions. Some pet stores sell an insecticide product that can be used to cure this disease.

Dropsy, Bloating, Ascites

You may find that one or more of your fish are bloated, showing a very swollen belly. There are three common reasons this occurs: The fish may be a female that is filled with eggs (or babies if it is a livebearer), it may simply be overfed, or it could have dropsy. Dropsy is a serious condition where the fish's kidneys are damaged and fluid begins to build up in the abdomen. The main distinguishing symptom is that in dropsy, the fish's scales tend to protrude

from the body rather than lie flat. Dropsy cannot be cured and rarely goes away on its own. You may need to consider euthanizing the fish if it has this disease. Luckily, dropsy is not contagious.

External Bacterial Diseases

Aquarium water is a virtual soup of different types of bacteria. Some are beneficial, but others can cause disease. Healthy fish are able to fend off attacks from these bacteria, but a fish that has damaged fins or skin may not be able to do so, and an infection may set in. Symptoms vary, but they are usually localized to the area of injury: white growths on the skin, eroded fins, cloudy eyes, and reddish streaks on the fish's body may all indicate a bacterial infection. In some cases, bacterial infections are secondary invaders after

Bloat, otherwise known as dropsy, is a serious condition that is very difficult to treat.

Dosing Medications

Some medications are dosed at "milligrams per liter," which is essentially the same as "parts per million." To calculate the amount of a drug needed in "ppm," you can use the following formula:

Multiply the target drug concentration in ppm by the tank volume in gallons and then divide this by 266. This gives the amount of drugs needed in grams. For example, if you needed to dose a 50-gallon aquarium with Praziquantel at 2 ppm, you would multiple 50 by 2 and divide by 266, which gives you 0.38 grams.

Sometimes you need to measure milliliters of a liquid drug. There are between 18 and 22 drops in a milliliter, and one teaspoon equals 5 milliliters.

another disease has already infected the fish. The best treatment is a general, broad-spectrum antibiotic effective against gram-negative bacteria. This will treat the most common bacterial fish diseases. Remember to remove the activated carbon from your filter, as this material will remove antibiotics from the water.

Treatment for bacterial diseases are difficult because you may end up harming your beneficial bacteria with the same treatment used to treat the disease. It is always a good idea to monitor your aquarium's ammonia level for a week or so following a treatment with antibiotics.

Flukes, Trematodes

Fish can become infected with tiny worms that live on their skin or gills. If the infestation becomes severe enough, the fish may die. Good tank conditions go a long way in helping the fish battle this disease on their own; poor water quality and overcrowding make the disease much more serious. Treatment includes a medication called

Praziquantel, dosed as per the label directions, or at a rate of 2.0 ppm, with two treatments, 10 days apart.

Fungus, Cotton Wool Disease, Water Mold (*Saprolegnia*)

Fungal infections look like little tufts of cotton wool on the fish's body or fins. Fungus only grows on dead tissue, so when you see this on a fish, it means it has suffered some injury. Your primary treatment is to identify the source of the injury (such as another fish attacking it) and make sure that the problem is resolved. The fungus itself actually serves to clean dead tissue out of a wound, and many people feel it should be left alone and not treated. If the fish is not too severely injured, it will recover. Eliminating the fungus may just open the wound to an even more serious bacterial infection.

Ich (Ick), White Spot Disease (*Ichthyophthirius*)

This is the most common disease in home aquariums. If not treated, it is capable of killing whole tanks of fish within a week or two. Luckily, there are medications available to treat this scourge, and if caught early enough, it rarely causes any fish losses. Ich often breaks out if the fish are chilled, or if they are stressed by a move. Watch out for ich on fish you have just brought home from the pet store. It is most commonly seen in the fall and spring months, probably due to changing temperatures in the outdoor ponds where many fish are raised.

Watch closely for the first symptoms: clamped fins, lethargy, and shimmying (wagging back and forth without moving forward). The next symptom is tiny white spots that show up on the fish's fins and body, looking like grains of salt. The spots may come and go over a day or two, but each time they return, there are more of them. It is vital to begin a treatment while the fish still have only a few spots. The reason is that the ich medications only affect the parasite at one stage of its life cycle, and each time the parasite multiplies, many hundreds of young are produced. If you are even a day late in starting the treatment, you may lose some fish. It is always a good idea to have a container of ich medication on hand so you don't have to delay the treatment taking time to get some from the store.

Low Dissolved Oxygen

If the amount of oxygen dissolved in the water is not high enough, the fish will begin to breathe more rapidly than normal. If the oxygen level goes lower still, fish will be seen gasping at the surface. Not all fish have the same dissolved oxygen requirements. Bettas, gouramis, and some catfish can take a breath of air directly from the surface and extract the oxygen from it. These fish will be unaffected by low dissolved oxygen levels in the water, so watch for symptoms in other species such as livebearers, tetras, and danios. If you suspect low oxygen levels, try to determine what has changed. Adding supplemental aeration from an air pump and airstone will provide relief within minutes. If the gasping symptoms continue, the cause may be a gill disease or some toxin in the water.

Protozoan Diseases

There are other single-celled organisms related to the "ich" parasite that can infect fishes. Three species are sometimes

Ich is easily recognized by the tiny white spots that cover the fish's fins and body.

Goldfish with swim bladder problems can sometimes be cured by feeding them crushed canned peas.

seen: *Chilodonella, Costia,* and *Trichodina.* Unlike the typical white spots seen in ich, infections of these protozoans only give vague symptoms, such as poor appetite, shimmying in place, or pale coloration. Without a microscope, it is impossible to diagnosis these diseases with any certainty. If you suspect your fish have this problem, and especially if some fish have already died, you may want to try treating the tank with a good general ich medication, but be forewarned that this "shotgun" approach does not always work.

Swim Bladder Disease

A fish may develop an infection or some other problem with its swim bladder. It will be unable to control its buoyancy, either sinking to the bottom or floating helpless at the surface. In most cases, if the fish does not get better on its own within two weeks, it should be euthanized. One exception is fancy goldfish. For some reason, they can sometimes be cured of this problem if fed crushed canned peas as part of their diet.

Tumors, Growths

Fish do develop tumors, especially as they get older. Some tumors are benign and don't cause any real harm, whereas others are malignant and spread to other tissues. There is no real treatment for this problem, so just observe the fish's general health and consider euthanizing it if it seems to be suffering.

Velvet (*Amyloodinium*)

This single-celled parasite shows up as a light dusting, sometimes brown in color, along the fish's back. It is often seen on gouramis and bettas, but other fish can develop it as well. It does not kill the fish as quickly as ich does, but it still needs to be treated. Try using a good ich medication, as well as increasing the aeration to the tank.

Aquarium and Equipment Maintenance

In order to keep your aquarium operating properly, it requires regular maintenance. Skipping aquarium maintenance tasks is the same as not changing the oil in your car—you can get away with it for a time, but eventually a serious problem will develop. A scheduled routine is the best way to keep on top of the maintenance needs of your aquarium.

Daily and Weekly Maintenance

You should inspect your aquarium at least once a day. Check the filter for proper operation and see that the water temperature is within the proper range. This is easily done at the same time you feed your fish. If something doesn't look quite right, stop and think it through. You may be noticing the start of a problem that could become more serious later on.

Water in an aquarium will evaporate and need to be replaced. The rate of evaporation depends on how well the aquarium is aerated, how it is covered, and the humidity in the room where the aquarium is located. An aquarium that is heavily aerated, has an open mesh cover, and is located in a dry, air-conditioned room is going to evaporate very fast. Such tanks may need to be topped up every few days. Well-covered aquariums may only need to be topped up once a week. Letting an aquarium evaporate down too far can cause the

Check your aquarium at least once a day to make sure everything is working properly.

filter or heater to malfunction. The easiest way to top up an aquarium is to simply add enough dechlorinated tap water, the same temperature as the tank, to bring the water back up to the proper level.

Algae is a photosynthetic plant-like organism that frequently grows on aquarium gravel, decorations, and on the sides of the aquarium. Beginning aquarium keepers often equate algae growth with dirt, but it is harmless and some fish get extra nutrition from grazing on it. Pet stores sell a variety of "algae eaters" that are purported to clean your aquarium of unwanted algae. Very few of them do a good job at this task, and in some cases, they may eat one type of algae, only to have it replaced by a growth of another species of algae

that the algae eater doesn't feed on. Algae control is usually a task for the aquarium keeper. Algae can be removed from the tank sides using various algae scrapers. Remember to always select the correct tool—soft acrylic aquariums can be scratched if you use a scraper designed for glass aquariums. Algae almost always starts off as a soft, easily removable growth that over time becomes thicker and much harder to remove. For that reason, you should wipe down the inside of the aquarium weekly with a soft cloth to keep the harder-to-remove algae from having time to form.

The outside glass of the aquarium will need to be cleaned from

Algae can be scraped off the glass on a regular basis using an algae scraper.

Calling in the Reinforcements

There will be times where your aquarium will experience a problem and you simply won't be able to figure out a solution. This happens to everyone at one time or another. This book will offer you solutions to all of the common problems, but if you get stuck, there are other resources you can look into.

Your local pet store can be a great source of additional information. You should start by contacting the store where you bought the fish or equipment you are having a problem

with. While the telephone seems the fastest and most convenient way to reach the store, it is usually better to make a visit. Bringing a sample of water and a picture of the aquarium in operation is usually very helpful.

Your local aquarium club, while probably not well suited for answering immediate questions (because they only meet once a month), is a great resource for long-term support of your aquariums.

Online forums may not be the best way to get your questions answered. First, the people helping you may not be any more experienced than you are, even if they sound like they really know what they are talking about. Second, they do not have access to information about your tank other than what you write. If you miss an important symptom, they won't know. Third, you will often receive conflicting answers from many different people, and you will have difficulty figuring out whose advice to follow.

Other books can be good resources for aquarium information. Check the publication dates, especially in library books, because much has changed in aquarium keeping in the past 25 years or so and you want to get the most up-to-date information possible.

Finally, your local veterinarian or public aquarium may be able to help you solve the really tricky problems.

time to time. A cloth and regular glass cleaner works well for glass tanks, but acrylic and other plastic tanks will require a soft cloth to keep them from being scratched. In addition, glass cleaners can harm some plastic tanks, so follow the manufacturer's recommendations. Never spray a cleaning material directly on an aquarium. The spray may travel up the side of the tank and get into the water, possibly harming the fish. A much better method is to stand away from the tank and spray a bit of the cleaner onto the cloth and use that to wipe down the outside of the aquarium. Remember to rinse your hands in tap water after this if you are planning to work inside the tank.

Water Changes

Although the beneficial bacteria break down the dangerous fish wastes ammonia and nitrite as fast as they are produced, other waste products do build up in aquarium water. Although much less toxic, they can eventually cause your fish problems if they are not removed. The best way to remove them is through what is called a *partial water change*. To do this, you physically remove some water from the aquarium and replace it with dechlorinated water of the proper temperature. One way

Family Fun

Yes, cleaning aquariums can be a bit of a chore at times, but dividing up the work between family members can really help. Besides, helping to clean aquariums teaches young people about the responsibilities of pet ownership.

to remove water from an aquarium is to start a siphon from the tank to a bucket on the floor. Never start a siphon by mouth. A safer way is to submerge the hose in the aquarium, place a finger over one end, and direct that end into the bucket. The other end must remain completely under water. When you take your finger off the end of the hose,

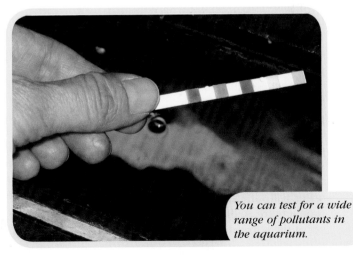

You can test for a wide range of pollutants in the aquarium.

A Word to the Wise

The water you add to an aquarium due to evaporation should not be counted as a water change, as only pure water leaves the tank during evaporation and all the fish wastes are left behind. These wastes need to be diluted by actually removing them with the water during a water change.

a siphon will start, with tank water flowing into the bucket. Water can be removed from smaller aquariums by dipping it out with a clean cup.

There is no set rule for how much or how often to change the water. A general rule of thumb is to change 25 percent of the water every week. A lightly stocked aquarium may be fine receiving a 30 percent water change every two weeks. What happens if you miss doing a water change? Nothing at all, at first. But if you miss a number of water changes, the water will become more and more polluted over time. Large water changes of 50 percent or more of the aquarium's volume can be stressful to the fish if not done with great care.

Advanced aquarists can measure the buildup of some of these waste products using special test kits. Nitrate and phosphorus are two common pollutants that build up in aquarium water. For regular home aquariums, though, simply measuring the pH of the water will suffice. Most of the waste products are acidic and will cause the pH of the aquarium's water to gradually

drop. A drop in pH of more than 1.5 units from its starting point means that more frequent water changes are required. For example, if the water from your tap has a pH of 8.5 and after a few months your aquarium's pH has dropped below 7.0, more frequent water changes are required. Another way to test for pollution is to take a tall clear glass of tank water and a tall glass of tap water and set them side by side on a piece of white paper. Looking down on them, if the tank water looks

Tank Volume Calculations

Don't just guess at how much water to take out for a water change or when dosing a medication. You can easily calculate the true volume of your tank.

For rectangular aquariums, measure the inside's length, width, and height (from the water's surface to the top of the gravel) in inches and multiply the three numbers together and divide by 231. This gives you the volume of your aquarium in gallons. If your tank has large rock decorations that displace some of the water, you may need to reduce this figure by 5 or 10 percent.

distinctly more yellow than the tap water, it may indicate the need for more frequent changes. Some people try to cut corners and reduce the number of water changes they perform by changing more water at one time. This can cause undue stress to the fish due to rapid changes in water chemistry and should only be done in an emergency.

If you have an odd-shaped aquarium, there are online calculators you can use to figure out the volume of cylinders or spheres. For multi-sided aquariums, try imagining the tank as a series of triangles. Fit them together to form rectangles and then calculate as above.

Siphon Cleaning

Over time, the gravel layer at the bottom of the aquarium tends to build up a lot of solid waste and uneaten food. This material is unsightly and can cause water pollution problems if it builds up. The best way to remove this *detritus* is through the use of a siphon cleaning device. These are simply siphon hoses with a large-diameter tube at one end. They are started just like a regular siphon, but then you gently move the large-diameter tube down into the gravel layer. The gravel is picked up by the water currents, but since the gravel is heavy, it drops back down while any lighter detritus continues on up the hose and out of the tank into the waste bucket. This procedure does takes some practice—if you work too slowly, you won't have time to go over all of the aquarium's gravel before the allotted amount of water has been removed. If you work too quickly and jam the end of the cleaner down into the gravel, it can clog.

Equipment Maintenance

Power filters will need to have their filter media changed on a regular basis. Most people find that changing or cleaning the filter media every two weeks is sufficient, and they often do this on a schedule opposite of the biweekly water changes. Follow the manufacturer's instructions if they differ and always watch your filter's output, as reduced flow usually indicates a need to change the media. Power filters that have magnetic impellers need to be disassembled, and the impeller chamber should be cleaned every few months. If the filter chatters loudly when you restart it, the bushings on the impeller are becoming worn and need to be replaced.

Aquarium heaters typically do not require any maintenance (other than checking them daily for proper operation) and are more reliable nowadays, but they were notorious for failing in either the "on" position (overheating the fish) or the "off" position (giving the fish a potentially fatal chill) in the past. Ask your pet store for recommendations on a good brand of heater to buy.

All mechanical devices wear out in time, and aquarium equipment is no exception. The problem is that this equipment is keeping your fish alive, so failure of an important part may cause serious problems. Advanced aquarium hobbyists usually have extra filters,

air pumps, and heaters on hand, so a failed piece of equipment can quickly be replaced. You need to determine for yourself if you will want to buy replacement equipment to have as

Scales All Around

It isn't only your fish that can have "scales."

Scale is a term used to describe a buildup of white calcium salts on hard surfaces exposed to water and then air. Frequently seen on bathroom sinks and shower surfaces, it can build up on the outside of aquariums as well. Many household products have been developed to remove scale deposits, but their safety is unknown for use around aquariums. One material that can be safely used to remove aquarium scale is white vinegar. Simply pour a small amount on a cloth and wipe down the scale buildup. The acidic vinegar will dissolve the alkaline calcium salts. Try not to let any vinegar get into the aquarium itself, but a drop or two won't harm the fish. If the scale is allowed to build up for a long time, it is much more difficult to remove. In those cases, there are special aquarium cleaning solutions that can be used.

Fish and Vacations

How do you take a vacation with your fish? Well, actually you don't; they would prefer to stay at home!

Seriously, when you go on vacation, you do need to make some preparations for your fish. First, change the power filter media and top the tank up. Feed the fish normally the day you leave, and use a timer for the tank lights. Your fish will be fine for 5 to 7 days like this.

If you will be gone longer, you may need to train somebody to come to your house and feed the fish and top up the tank to offset water lost due to evaporation. It is best to pre-measure the food for them into little cups for each feeding. Remember that almost everyone tends to overfeed fish if they are not very experienced.

If you are out of town a lot, you may want to invest in an electronic feeder that will place a set amount of food into the tank every day for you.

Do *not* feed the fish heavily before you leave in anticipation of them missing some meals. This can pollute the water, and fish do not store up food energy very well anyway.

spares, or if you will just hope that you'll be able to get to a pet store in time to buy a replacement if needed. Another helpful method for avoiding catastrophic equipment failure is to build redundancy in the system. Two small filters can serve the same size tank as one large filter can, but the chance of both filters failing at the same time, leaving the tank without filtration, is minimal. Likewise, two small heaters on a tank will not fail at the same time. If one of the heaters does fail, say in the "on" position, the other heater will turn off in response to the rising water temperature. This will reduce the degree that the water will overheat. These redundant systems do add to the cost of maintaining an aquarium. Perhaps the most cost-effective redundancy is to have both a power filter and an aeration device on the aquarium. That way, if either the filter or the air pump fails, the other device can maintain acceptable oxygen levels for the fish until you have time to fix things.

Aquarium Safety

The safety of any people who are in contact with your aquariums is very important. This means you need to work safely but also maintain an aquarium safe for family and friends as well. Small children need special protection from the potential dangers of aquariums. Never place an aquarium on a stand that is not secure; a child might be able to reach up and topple it over onto themselves. All fish

Always use a ground fault circuit interrupter outlet with aquarium equipment.

States. In other countries, you should look for products that are CE listed (which means that it conforms to European product standards).

Some other basic safety precautions are important:

Never work on an aquarium in bare feet or with wet shoes. Never touch an aquarium power cord, plug, or switch with your wet hands.

If you accidently drop a non-submersible electrical device into an aquarium, don't reach for it. Instead, unplug the item or turn off power to the room at the circuit breaker.

Never override the three-pronged ground on any plug used around water. Always use a ground fault circuit interrupter (GFCI) system to plug in any of your aquarium's electrical devices.

medications and water treatments must be locked up away from small children. This is also important from the standpoint of safety for the animals themselves—many small children want to "help out" by feeding the aquarium, often with disastrous results. It makes sense that all aquariums in homes with small children must be securely covered, and this includes any vats, buckets, and tubs used to hold water for water changes.

Concerns with Electricity

Water and electricity are a dangerous combination. Whenever possible, choose aquarium equipment that has been approved by the Underwriters Laboratory (UL listed) in the United

Proper Handling of Aquarium Chemicals

Some potentially dangerous chemicals are used in and around aquariums. Proper handling of any of these products is very important. Because aquarium chemicals are not intended for use with humans or for food animals, the product labeling requirements are minimal. Some products do not even list their active ingredients. Treat all unknown products with care, and keep all chemicals out of the reach of children.

Dangerous Aquarium Animals

There are some species of aquatic animals that can harm people. The majority of these, such as lionfish and

Be sure to place all chemicals, medications, and fish food in an area out of reach of children.

blue ring octopus, are only seen by marine aquarium keepers. Still, there are a few concerns, even for beginning freshwater aquarium keepers.

Never place anything that has been in an aquarium into your mouth (the most common problem is when people try to start a siphon with their mouth). There are bacterial diseases you can catch if you get aquarium water in your mouth. Always wash your hands thoroughly before and after handling your aquarium animals, their water, or any uncooked fish foods.

Until you have researched the animal's habits, consider any new aquatic species you are unfamiliar with as possibly being dangerous.

A variety of fish such as pacu, cichlids, and piranhas can bite. This is a misdirected feeding response, easily avoided by not placing your hands in the tank.

Stingrays and some catfish can inject venom through sharp spines (located on the tail in rays and at the front of the dorsal and pectoral fins in catfish). First aid for these wounds is to submerge the injury in the hottest water the person can stand, and then get medical attention if needed. Use caution when handling any fish, as even non-venomous fish can inject bacteria into you with their spines.

Maintaining Your Aquarium

Chapter 6

So Many Choices!

Species That Are a Bit More Challenging

There are literally thousands of species and varieties of fish and invertebrates available to home aquarium keepers. This chapter outlines some that have special requirements, are less compatible, or that are more challenging than the species listed in the previous chapter. There are certain types of fish that really should not be kept by home aquarists at all, and these are listed at the end of the chapter.

You Can Judge a Fish by its Fins

You can sometimes use the way a fish looks to predict how it will behave in an aquarium:

Mouth location: Fish with downturned mouths feed from the bottom, those with upturned mouths feed from the surface. Mouth size is also important – a fish with an ear-to-ear grin is likely able to swallow some other fish!

Tail shape: Fish with forked tails are usually fast, open water swimmers. Fish with rounded tails are slower, but much more maneuverable. A fish with a squared off tail can swim pretty fast, but can still easily change course.

Body shape: Long eel shapes allow a fish to swim between rocks and other tight places. A long straight body means the fish is a fast open water swimmer. Fish that spend a lot of time in one place usually have a chunky body.

Eye size: Fish with large eyes are often more active at night. If the pupil of a fish's eye is elongated at the front, they are often predators (the stretched pupil helps them track fast moving prey).

Coloration: Fish with lighter bellies are usually open water swimmers – it makes it harder for predators to see them from below. Fish with camouflaged colors are either trying to hide from predators – or if they also have a large mouth, are trying to hide from their prey until they can get close enough to eat them. If males of a species are more brightly colored than the females, they are trying to attract attention. During breeding season, these colorful males may fight one another.

Fish that don't seem to have any outstanding differences in the way they look are usually "generalists" and don't have any single outstanding talent, but can do a number of things fairly well.

Try predicting the habits of fish you see in pictures in books – then read about them and see if you are right!

Cichlids

There are over 1300 species of cichlids found around the world, mostly in South America and Africa. They range in size from 2-inch (5-cm) dwarf cichlids to monsters of the genus *Cichla* that reach close to 3 feet (1 meter) in length. Some, such as angelfish, are great beginner's fish, but most are larger and more aggressive. Some generalizations can be made of typical cichlids; they tend to uproot aquatic plants, are territorial, and grow larger than typical community tank fish. They also have more personality than most fish, which makes them very popular with many aquarists.

One curious note about the territorial nature of cichlids is that a few in an aquarium may fight to the death, but if a large number are added to the aquarium at the same time, the aggression toward any one fish is limited and no fish comes to harm. Of course, care must be taken in doing this to avoid overloading the biological filter! Cichlids do well on prepared foods; in fact, there are many pelleted foods designed just for these fish. Some cichlids from the Rift Lakes of Africa prefer hard, alkaline water, while species from South America may require soft, acidic water. There is even a species of cichlid called a tilapia that can survive in seawater.

Native Fishes

Many people have wondered about catching their own fish locally and keeping them in an aquarium. While this is a popular side hobby, it does have some special considerations. In most areas, you are required to have a fishing license in order to catch any fish for your home aquariums. In addition, it is illegal to catch and keep game fish such as bass or pike if they are smaller than what the fishing laws of the region allow. Many native fish grow larger than what can be comfortably housed in a typical home aquarium. Finally, many native fish are just not as brightly colored as their tropical counterparts, and those that are tend to only show their colors during the breeding season. Native fishes from temperate climates (such as those found in many regions of the US) need to be kept in cooler water than tropical fishes, so these animals should not be mixed in the same aquarium. If you want to go native, you should

stick with just those species and not try to mix them with tropical types.

Aggressive Fish

There are some species of fish that are so aggressive, or so highly predatory, that they cannot easily be kept with any other fish. Aquarium keepers interested in these species may decide to set up a single-species tank to house them. Be forewarned that the lack of diversity in such tanks can lead to the aquarist quickly becoming bored with them. Many people think it would be really cool to have a school of piranhas (*Pygocentrus nattereri*) in their aquarium, but they soon realize that these fish are just big tetras and are actually pretty uninteresting to watch.

Other single-species tanks might house an *Aba aba* knifefish or a big jaguar cichlid (*Parachromis managuensis*). Snakeheads (*Channa* spp.) were once popular single-species aquarium fish, but they are now illegal in the US for fear that they will be released and then survive as invasive

Kribs are cichlids that are relatively easy to keep and don't get very large.

Some Native Fishes for Home Aquariums

Darters (*Etheostoma* spp.) prefer cool, oxygenated water and live foods. They are bottom dwelling.
Flagfish (*Jordanella floridae*) are very hardy and will eat algae. They are raised in fish farms for aquariums.
Madtoms (*Noturus* spp.) are small catfish that can sting. They hide under rocks during the day.
Minnows (*Notropis* spp.) are similar to danios, but they are only colorful during breeding season.
Mosquitofish (*Gambusia* spp.) are similar to guppies but more aggressive.
Pygmy sunfish (*Elassoma* spp.) are tiny and very shy. They require live food and plants to hide in.
Stickleback (*Culaea inconstans*) prefer live food such as *Daphnia*, and they have sharp dorsal spines.
Sunfish (*Lepomis* spp.) are similar to cichlids in their habits and can be aggressive.
Topminnows (*Fundulus* spp.) are similar to swordtails in their habits and are surface dwellers.

care requirements, so always research a new fish carefully before buying it.

African Butterflyfish (*Pantodon buchholzi*)

These brown fish have long banded pectoral fins that resemble leaves when you look down on them as they float near the surface. They are excellent jumpers and grow to a length of around 4 inches (10 cm). In the wild, they prey on insects that fall onto the surface of the water. Crickets are an excellent starter food, but most butterflyfish adapt to feeding on soft floating foods like freeze-dried tubifex or brine shrimp.

Bichirs (*Polypterus* spp.)

A prehistoric group of fish from Africa, the bichirs (or reedfish) are popular fish for people with larger aquariums. They breathe air and are good escape artists, so their aquarium needs to be well covered, yet still giving them access to some air. These carnivorous fish do best when fed meaty foods such as shrimp pieces, large krill, and whole frozen fish such as silversides. Although slow moving, they are able to catch and eat smaller fish at night.

species in local waters (which has already happened around the Potomac River).

Oddballs

From time to time, pet stores may offer some real oddball species for sale. Many of these have special

Flagfish are a colorful species of native fish that eat algae in aquariums.

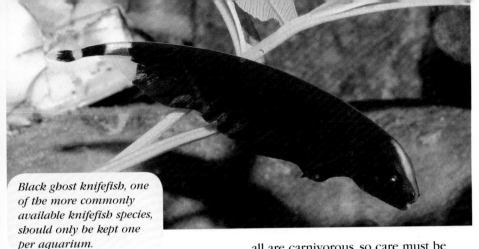

Black ghost knifefish, one of the more commonly available knifefish species, should only be kept one per aquarium.

Elephantnose Fish (*Gnathonemus* and Related Species)

These African fish are named for the long snouts possessed by some species. Related fish without snouts are often sold as "baby whales" due to their large heads and gray, scaleless bodies. All members of the group are good jumpers. They are shy during the day and require a cave to hide in. Elephantnose fish have weak electrical organs they use to navigate at night and possibly to communicate with one another. As a group, they almost always refuse to feed on flake or pellet foods, requiring instead a variety of live or frozen food items such as brine shrimp, tubifex worms, or even diced earthworms.

Knifefish (*Notopterus* and Related Species)

These elongated fish have a single long fin along their underside that they ripple to move forward or backward. Many species grow quite large, and all are carnivorous, so care must be taken when housing them with smaller fish. Some knifefish are also highly territorial, and one per aquarium may be the safest way to go.

Silver Dollars (*Metynnis* and Related Species)

These large silver tetras are actually in the same group as the piranha but are unique in that they are vegetarian and will leave other fish alone (but will, of course, eat live aquarium plants). There are a wide variety of flake and pelleted foods with extra plant material added that work very well as a staple diet for silver dollars. The closely related pacu should be avoided because they grow too large for virtually any home aquarium.

Spiny Eel (*Mastacembelus* Species)

Not true eels, these elongated fish are popular with some aquarium keepers. The beautiful fire eel reaches a length of nearly 3 feet (91 cm) while the more common tire-track eel only attains half that size. Well known for their ability to

Designer Fish

People frequently try to improve on nature. With fish, this has mainly been through selective breeding, where fish breeders select offspring that have desirable traits such as brighter colors and longer fins. By breeding those fish together, they get some that have even longer fins or even brighter colors. With perseverance, new varieties of fish can be developed. Some people don't appreciate these unnatural fish while others do; it is really a matter of personal taste. However, there are other ways that people have been trying to enhance their fish, and some of these methods may not be appropriate.

Albino fish: A natural mutation, albino fish in the wild are often eaten by predators because they stand out so much. In captivity, this mutation can be reinforced, and a strain of albino fish can be developed. A true albino will have pink or red eyes. A leucocystic fish may be light in color, but it will have blue or black eyes.

Dyed fish: Clear or light-colored fish can be painted or injected with organic dyes to have different colors on their bodies. Sometimes fish are given special seasonal dye jobs, such as painted-on red hearts around Valentine's Day. The extra handling required to dye these fish can leave them weakened and susceptible to disease. The dye wears off in a few months anyway, and you end up with a regular-looking fish. Always avoid buying these fish.

Intergenus crossbreeding: For thousands of years, people have crossbred closely related species to produce hybrids. Sometimes these hybrids have attributes that make them stronger or larger than either of the parent species. Some people have been artificially crossbreeding fish from different genera, which are not closely related, to produce bizarre hybrids. This is sometimes done with giant South American catfish. Avoid these fish, as you will end up with a hybrid that will grow too large for your aquarium anyway!

Parrot cichlid: This strange-looking fish was apparently developed by crossbreeding three or four different cichlid species. Their bodies and mouths are deformed into a shape that some people find attractive but others do not. They are sometimes dyed, which makes them even more of a fish to be avoided.

Transgenic fish: GloFish® were developed by introducing genetic material from a jellyfish into zebra danio fish. The offspring of these fish carry the same gene, and they glow under actinic or black lighting. These fish are only available in the US (except California) under license from the original developer. It is against the law to sell transgenic organisms in Australia, Canada, or the European Union.

Avoid buying fish that have been artificially injected with dye, such as these glassfish, as the treatment can be quite harmful to them.

An aquarium containing a newt needs to be tightly covered to prevent escapes.

escape aquariums, some spiny eels can also burrow under the aquarium gravel, causing the aquarium keeper to look around the floor for an escaped fish, only to discover it later as it pokes its long nose from under the gravel.

Upside-Down Catfish (*Synodontis nigriventris*)
These larger but peaceful catfish come from Africa. As its name implies, this species spends much of its time feeding upside down at the surface. This change for the normal bottom-dwelling habit seen in other catfish is probably an adaptation to the waters where it lives. Being at the surface gives the fish better access to oxygen, as well as first dibs on any food item that hits the surface.

Amphibians
While most are better suited for terrariums, there are a few species of amphibians that will do well in aquariums. Amphibians differ from fish in that they lack scales and most have legs. Most amphibians breathe air, but some have gills or can absorb oxygen from the water through their skin.

African Dwarf Frog
African dwarf frogs of the genus *Hymenochirus* are truly aquatic. They do not need land to bask on like most other frogs and live their entire life in water. They can reach a length of 2.5 inches (6.4 cm). They may eat baby fish and some larger fish may pester them, but they are otherwise compatible aquarium inhabitants. They prefer meaty food items such as bloodworms, brine shrimp, or small cut-up earthworms. A similar species, the African clawed frog (*Xenopus* sp.), grows larger and is aggressive toward many species of fish. Telling these species apart is simple—the more desirable dwarf frog has webbing between the digits of its front legs and the clawed frog does not.

Crystal red shrimp have been selectively bred for their vibrant coloration.

Newts

The oriental fire-bellied newt (*Cynops* sp.) is occasionally offered for sale in pet stores. They are escape artists, so their aquarium must be tightly covered. Newts also prefer slightly cooler water temperatures than tropical fish, generally less than 75°F (24°C). This species reaches a length of 4 inches (10 cm) and prefers meaty foods like frozen bloodworms but will sometimes take sinking pelleted food. It should be mentioned that these newts have toxic skin secretions, so keep them away from pets or small children and wash your hands after handling them.

Invertebrates

There are a few invertebrates (animals without backbones) suitable for freshwater aquariums. Two points to understand are that fish often feed on small invertebrates, and some fish medications will kill invertebrates. With that in mind, some aquarium keepers may find adding invertebrates to their aquarium adds quite a bit of diversity.

Clams

Asian freshwater clams (*Corbicula* sp.) are sometimes sold for aquarium use. They are sometimes sold as "living filters" because they take in water and filter out organic material. Remember, though, that they produce waste themselves, so they really do not make your aquarium any cleaner. They spend all of their time buried in the sand or gravel at the bottom of the tank, with just their siphons visible. Do not add clams to a newly set-up aquarium because it takes time for enough organic material to build up for them to feed on.

Crabs

Various species of crabs are sold for freshwater aquariums, but most are actually brackish-water animals that do not thrive in freshwater aquariums. A few species are true freshwater animals, but they can be aggressive toward each other and toward fish. Most crabs are avid climbers and will escape from the aquarium unless it is very well covered. Unless you want to set up a half-level aquarium just for them, it is best to avoid crabs.

Crayfish

These large crustaceans of the genus *Cherax* and *Procambarus* resemble miniature lobsters. Some species are territorial and require a larger aquarium if more than one will be kept. Other species are prone to grabbing and eating small fish. It is best to ask your dealer for advice concerning the species they have for sale. These crayfish are scavengers and will feed readily on sinking pelleted foods. Like all crustaceans, they molt (shed their skin) as they grow.

Shrimp

Dwarf shrimp of the genus *Caridina*, such as the Amano and crystal red shrimp, have become incredibly popular in recent years. Some of these shrimp have been selectively bred to develop more vibrant colors. Most of these shrimp are omnivores and will feed on algae, as well as finely powdered flake foods. Because of their small size and peaceful nature, they are not normally kept in aquariums with fish, although some very small fish species may cohabitate with them. Bamboo shrimp (*Atyopsis* sp.) are filter feeders and require the addition of finely powdered foods or a well-established aquarium in order to thrive.

Snails

A wide variety of snails are available for freshwater aquariums. Most feed on algae while some consume uneaten food. A few species will eat live aquarium plants, so check with your

Popular Snails for Home Aquariums

Apple Snails	Mystery Snails	Ramshorn Snails	Malaysian Snails
Has lung and gill	Has gill only	Has gill only	Has lung and gill
Won't eat plants	Won't eat plants	Will eat plants	May eat plants
Lays eggs in hard shells above water's surface	Broods young internally, does not lay eggs	Lays eggs in gelatinous mass underwater	Broods young internally, does not lay eggs
Very large species	Many color types	Requires hard water	Can become a pest

A Few Fish
That Beginning Aquarium Keepers
Might Also Want to Avoid

There are some species of fish commonly sold in pet stores that can make good aquarium inhabitants but which beginning aquarium keepers should still avoid. Later on, after you've gained some experience and know more about fishkeeping, these would make better choices.

Black tetra (*Gymnocorymbus ternetzi*): Although this species is hardy and inexpensive, they are often a bit too rough on other, more peaceful fish in smaller aquariums.

Cardinal tetra (*Paracheirodon axelrodi*): Arguably the prettiest freshwater fish, the cardinal and neon tetras are a bit more delicate than some people might expect. They do best in a tank with other peaceful fish, live plants, and with soft water having a low pH.

Chinese algae eater (*Gyrinocheilus aymonieri*): Although commonly sold as a beginner's fish, this species grows large and tends to chase other fish in the aquarium. To make matters worse, despite its name, it does not feed on enough algae to make an aquarium look any nicer.

Common plecostomus (*Hypostomus* spp.): These grow much larger than most people realize. While relatively peaceful, a plecostomus can quickly outgrow a 50-gallon aquarium. Their ability to eat unwanted algae is also overrated.

Hatchetfish (*Gasteropelecus* spp.): Although very unique looking, these fish are well known for their ability to jump out of aquariums, even those with covers. Because these species are wild collected, they often arrive stressed out from their long journey. They also do best if fed live or freeze-dried food rather than regular fish flakes.

Molly (*Poecilia* spp.): This is another commonly sold fish that doesn't always do well for beginners. Mollies require hard water with a bit of salt in it. More importantly, they prefer food that has a substantial amount of plant material in it (such as algae).

Tinfoil barb (*Barbonymus schwanenfeldii*): Commonly sold as juveniles about 1.5 inches (3.8 cm) long, many people don't realize that these fish grow much larger than other types of barbs, easily reaching a length of 11 inches (28 cm) and will require at least a 100-gallon (380-liter) aquarium.

dealer if you intend to keep both snails and plants together.

Fishes to Avoid

There are some species of fish that are just not suitable for being kept by most home aquarists. They may be offered for sale in stores, but if your experience level or aquarium size is not adequate for their proper care, you should steer clear of them.

There are different reasons why these species are not for beginning aquarists.

1. Some species, such as butterfly "gobies" (*Vespicula depressifrons*) and freshwater stingrays (*Potamotrygon* spp.) can harm an aquarist with venomous spines or sharp teeth. Extreme care must be taken when handling venomous animals.

2. Some species have strict requirements that cannot be met in a basic home aquarium. Examples are fish that only eat certain exotic foods or need very special water conditions. A few of these fish to avoid are chocolate gouramis (*Sphaerichthys osphromenoides*) and "freshwater" morays (*Echidna rhodochilus*).

3. There are species endangered in the wild that should not be purchased to help preserve wild populations. These include arapaima (*Arapaima gigas*), Asian arowana (*Scleropages formosus*), and freshwater stingrays.

4. Many species may be quite hardy but quickly outgrow the largest home aquarium. A sampling of these species are arapaima, Asian arowanas, arowanas (*Osteoglossum* spp.), freshwater stingrays, giant catfish (for example, the redtail and shovelnose), giant gouramis (*Osphronemus goramy*), iridescent sharks (*Pangasius* sp.), pacu (*Colossoma* spp.), snakeheads (*Channa* spp., illegal in the US), and sturgeon (*Acipenser* spp.).

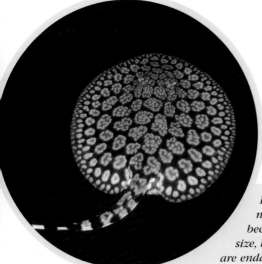

Freshwater stingrays should not be kept in aquariums because they grow to a very large size, have a venomous spine, and are endangered in the wild.

Chapter 7

Advancing in the Hobby

So now that you have a properly functioning aquarium, you can just sit back and simply enjoy the fish you have—or perhaps not! Many people find the aquarium hobby so intriguing that they set up a second, third, or even more aquariums! If you're interested in moving from a single freshwater aquarium to more involvement with aquariums as a hobby, this chapter will help show you the way.

Breeding Fishes

Probably no other aspect of the aquarium hobby is as rewarding as breeding the fish in your aquarium. Keeping your fish alive and healthy is one thing, but actually creating conditions favorable enough that baby fish are produced is much more interesting. For many beginning aquarists, there is an aura of mystery surrounding raising aquarium fish (especially egg-laying species), but this is really just caused by a lack of good information. Once armed with some basic information and a little extra effort, every home aquarium keeper can be successful in raising at least some species of fish.

The first step is to decide what species of fish you want to breed and then research the requirements to do so. It is important to first make sure that you have homes for any baby fish you produce. For example, the convict cichlid (*Amatitlania nigrofasciata*) is an easily bred egg-laying species, but as adults, they are fairly aggressive and few people have tanks suitable to house them. As a result, it would be very difficult for you to find good homes for 100 or so baby convict cichlids. On the other hand, pet stores sell hundreds of angelfish a month and are almost always on the lookout for good-quality angelfish to sell.

The usual reason people fail in raising their aquarium fish is not in getting their fish to spawn or the eggs

Five Important Factors for Breeding Fish in Aquariums

1	Make sure you have a compatible pair.	You need a pair of fish to start with. It is not always easy to tell males from females, and some pairs are not compatible.
2	Be certain they are healthy. Ensure they have proper environmental conditions.	Is the tank large enough? Is the water clean and of the proper temperature?
3	Feed the pair of fish well on a variety of foods.	Always feed some live foods if possible. This often gets fish to spawn.
4	Give them proper light/ temperature cycles.	Some fish require environmental triggers to get them to spawn. Research the species you are trying to breed.
5	Don't breed fish in excess of your needs.	You are responsible for ensuring you have good future homes for any fish you produce.

to hatch but in supplying the proper food to feed the larval fish. Aquarium keepers are so used to just opening a jar of store-bought food to feed their fish that they are not prepared to raise their own microscopic foods needed by the baby fish. The two main foods for baby freshwater fish are *infusoria* and live baby brine shrimp (*Artemia*).

Breeding fish can be an enjoyable yet challenging pastime.

Live baby brine shrimp is easy enough to hatch from dry eggs, but infusoria requires a bit more effort. Infusoria is just a growth of microscopic algae and protozoans. The culture needs to be set up well in advance of the time it will be needed. First, a series of small jars are set up in a sunny window. Then an airstone is added to each container along with a starter culture of infusoria and a food source. The starter culture can be a small bit of pond scum or a culture from another hobbyist. The food for these creatures may be a small bit of chopped hay, crumpled lettuce, or a teaspoon of dried pea soup. When the water turns a dark green, it's ready to use. Small amounts (3 or 4 tablespoons) of the infusoria culture are added to the fry tank throughout the day. After a few days, most baby fish have grown large enough to then start feeding on newly hatched brine shrimp.

Fish breeders often need to have a number of small aquariums as well as a few larger ones all operating at the same time. The larger tanks are for growing up groups of offspring, while the small tanks are used to house breeding pairs of fish or their larva. It helps if you consolidate all of these aquariums onto a single heavy-duty stand. This is less expensive and takes up much less space than having individual stands for each aquarium. Some people get so involved in fish breeding that they dedicate a room or portion of their

Baby brine shrimp can be hatched from dry eggs.

Fish That Are Good Candidates for Aquarium Breeding

Easy to breed:
- Livebearers: guppies, platies, and swordtails
- ~~Zebra danio (*Danio rerio*)~~

More difficult to breed:
- Angelfish
- Royal Farlowella catfish (*Sturisoma* spp.)
- Lake Tanganyikan cichlids: *Frontosa, Tropheus, Julidochromis*

Very difficult to breed:
- Discus
- *Corydoras* catfish
- Rainbowfish

trouble reproducing normally. It's best to start with breeding livebearers that more closely resemble their wild counterparts. The only other real difficulty in breeding livebearers is that the other fish (including the mother herself) can be cannibalistic and eat the young fish. For this reason, it is better to move the pregnant female fish to a livebearer breeding trap before she gives birth. When the babies are born, they sink down through a narrow gap where the mother cannot find them. After a day or two, you can assume that all the babies have been born and the mother can be returned to the tank. The babies can remain in the breeding tank or moved to their own small aquarium. Feeding the babies is easy—just crumble some fish flakes into tiny pieces (there are also special baby fish foods available). Once the babies are about one third the size of the adult fish, they can be safely returned to the main aquarium.

basement into a space just for these activities.

By far, the easiest fish to breed are livebearers such as guppies, platys, and swordtails. The male fish inserts his sperm into the female using a special fin called a gonopodium. The baby fish develop inside the female and are born alive after six to twelve weeks. The babies are termed precocious, in that they are ready to swim and eat regular aquarium food from the first day.

Many fancy varieties of livebearers have been developed through selective breeding. Some of these have such modified fins that the males have

Livebearers, which are easy to breed, have been selectively developed into an astounding array of shapes and colors.

Brackish-Water Aquariums

Where rivers run down to the sea, there are areas where fresh water and sea water mix. There are fish that are adapted to living in this unique region that is saltier than river water but not as salty as the ocean. Some of these *brackish-water* fish make interesting aquarium inhabitants. These aquariums are not quite as complicated as marine (saltwater) aquariums, but they do require some extra care in that the salt content needs to be monitored. Just like in a marine aquarium, the salt level is measured using a hydrometer. Salt water is denser than fresh water, and the hydrometer has a pointer that floats up or down depending on the amount of salt dissolved in the water. Most brackish water aquariums have a specific gravity (salt content) of 1.005 to 1.012. Fresh water has a specific

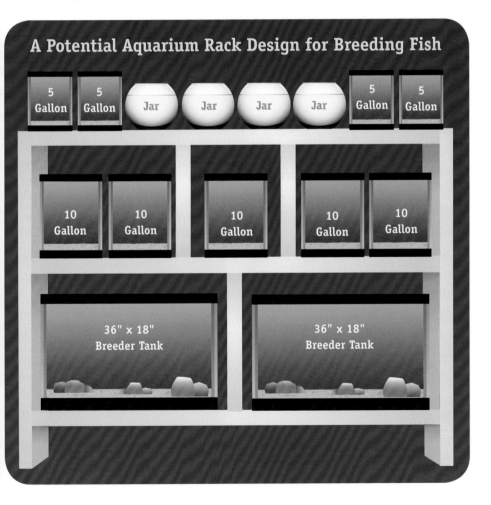

A Potential Aquarium Rack Design for Breeding Fish

Brackish-Water Fishes for Home Aquariums

Archerfish (*Toxotes jaculatrix*): Can spit water at insects
Black and sailfin mollies: Can live in fresh water to marine
Bumblebee goby (*Brachygobius* spp.): Colorful but small goby
Celebes rainbowfish (*Marosatherina ladigesi*): A delicate, peaceful fish
Colombian shark-cat (*Ariopsis seemanni*): Grows to over 3 feet (1 meter) long!
Dragon fish (*Gobioides broussonnetii*): A delicate species of goby
Fingerfish (*Monodactylus sebae*): Inhabits mangrove swamps
Four-eyed fish (*Anableps* spp.): Surface dweller, strange eyes
"Freshwater moray eel" (*Gymnothorax tile*): Actually a marine species, not suitable for freshwater.
"Freshwater lionfish" (*Batrachomoeus trispinosus*): A toadfish, will eat smaller fish
Glassfish (*Parambassis ranga*): Do not buy the fake-colored fish
Green scat (*Scatophagus argus*): Named for eating "scat" (poop)
Green spotted puffer (*Tetraodon* spp.): Mean, will bite fins of other fish
Moonfish/mono (*Monodactylus argenteus*): Hardy, graceful species
Mudskipper (*Periophthalmus* spp.): Needs shallow areas to breathe air
Orange chromide (*Etroplus maculatus*): A brackish-water cichlid from Asia
Siamese tigerfish (*Datnioides microlepis*): Grows large, highly predatory
Silver scat (*Selenotoca multifasciata*): A smaller species of scat
Sleeper goby (*Dormitator maculatus*): Grows large, but fairly peaceful

Mudskippers have very specialized requirements and will most likely need a tank of their own.

gravity of 1.000 while typical marine aquariums operate at 1.020 to 1.025.

Some of the fish available for brackish-water aquariums are similar to freshwater fish in their habits, while others are more like marine species. A few, like the mudskipper, have more specialized requirements and usually need a tank set up just for them. For the most part, these fish are all collected in the wild, and just like wild-caught freshwater fish, they may have a little extra difficulty adapting to the confines of home aquariums.

Marine Aquariums

Marine aquariums open up more of

the aquatic realm to home aquarists. Animals such as starfish, sea anemones, and octopuses can only be kept in marine aquariums. The marine aquarium hobby, although quite rewarding, can be expensive and time consuming, as well as frustrating to those people not willing to make the effort to learn the proper techniques.

The potential marine hobbyist should examine their motives for wanting a marine aquarium. If you truly wish to try and understand this small piece of the sea brought into your home and care for the animals in the best manner you can, this may be a hobby for you. On the other hand, if you are simply attracted to the beauty of marine animals and just wish to have a piece of "living furniture," then you might consider staying with the less demanding hobby of freshwater fishkeeping or perhaps investigate having an aquarium maintenance service properly care for your animals for you.

Fish-only marine aquariums differ from freshwater aquariums primarily in their need for a proper amount of salt in the water (most people use synthetic sea salts rather than ocean water). Another difference, though, is that with just a few exceptions, marine fish available to home aquarists were captured in the wild. This means that they have traveled thousands of miles to get to your home, and some of these fish do not make this transition very well. Finally, marine fish are more

Mini-reef aquariums typically have many more invertebrates than fish.

expensive. While nobody ever wants to lose a fish, having a $4 freshwater angelfish die in your aquarium is not as bad as having a $75 marine angelfish pass away in your tank.

A specific type of marine aquarium has become very popular in recent years. Termed "mini reefs," these aquariums focus less on fish and more on invertebrate life, mainly living stony and soft corals. While very beautiful and closely resembling a natural reef, they are more difficult to maintain than a fish-only marine tank. The water must be kept free of extra nutrients and waste products. One way to accomplish this is by frequent water changes (which gets expensive when you need to mix up synthetic sea salt that costs between 25 to 60 cents a gallon!). Another way to maintain good water quality is through something known as a protein skimmer (or foam fractionator). These devices inject air into a stream of water, producing

SMALL FRY

My First Job as a Gofer

My first job was as a *gofer* (as in, "you *go fer* this and *go fer* that") at a pet store in 1970. I fetched the owner's lunch, swept the floor, and took out the trash. I was paid $1.00 an hour or $1.20 an hour if I took my pay in trade for fish (which I almost always did!). There were four of us in this position, all trying to become "real" employees by showing the boss how hard we could work. As I recall, I was the third of the four gofers to eventually be promoted to cleaning tanks and catching fish for customers. All of this was of course contrary to child labor laws; we were 10 and 11 years old and couldn't have gotten work permits until we were 14. Still, we learned a lot about aquariums just by being around fish so much of the time. All through high school and college, I worked for local pet stores as a part-time job. With dozens of aquariums and fish of all types, I learned a lot more about aquariums working in pet stores than I ever could from my own home aquarium.

bubbles that are coated with waste products. When these bubbles burst, the waste is collected in a cup for later disposal.

Mini reefs also need to have trace elements and calcium added to the water because the corals remove these from the water as they grow. Most of the corals housed in these aquariums have a symbiotic algae called zoothanthellae that live in their tissues. This algae takes in light and produces simple sugars and other nutrients that the coral uses to grow. In turn, the algae gains protection from animals that might otherwise eat it because the coral has stinging cells like jellyfish. This means that to grow corals in captivity, the aquarium must be outfitted with special lights that produce enough energy, of the right spectrum, for the algae to grow. If this algae dies, so will the coral. These special lights can be expensive, and some use a lot of electricity. Still, despite the extra cost and effort, mini reefs are very popular with many marine aquarists.

Careers Working in Aquariums

Some people decide to take their aquarium hobby to the next level and actually make a career of working with fish in aquariums. Jobs working with aquariums range from a part-time job at a pet store to working as a professional aquarist for a large public aquarium. To get a job at a pet store, you need to learn what you can about keeping fish, plus be able to show that you are a hard worker and willing to learn. To get a job in a public aquarium, you'll need to learn how to scuba dive, have lots of aquarium experience, and usually a college degree in biology or a related field.

Career Focus During Elementary School

Even during elementary school, you can begin getting ready for junior and senior high school—and beyond! Visit your school library and read all you can about biology, fish, and aquariums. Learn to swim and how to snorkel, as these are skills you will need to become a good scuba diver later on. Obviously, a home aquarium (or two!) will give you the hands-on experience you will need for a career working with fish.

Middle School

Mathematics is very important at this age. Students who fail to progress past algebra at this point often have a difficult time catching up at a later date. Computer skills are generally best if self taught—kids seem to pick up this skill just fine if left to their own devices (but not too many computer games!).

At this age, you'll be able to operate your own aquarium and maybe even start taking scuba lessons (you usually need to be 14 years old to take these lessons). You should focus on doing well at school and reading all you can about aquariums and the aquatic environment. You may need a part-time job to help pay for your aquariums.

High School

Your coursework in high school should focus on college preparatory classes such as advanced biology, trigonometry, and physics. Now is the time to begin researching what colleges you may want to attend. Learning photography, electronics, and taking classes like

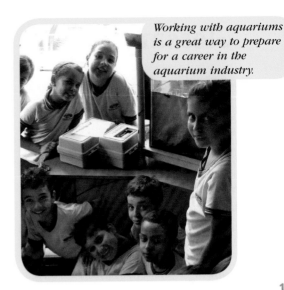

Working with aquariums is a great way to prepare for a career in the aquarium industry.

metal shop can also give you skills you can use later on. Joining a local aquarium club and working at local pet stores is advantageous for many high school students interested in aquariums as a career.

College

Only a few schools in the country offer classes that include training in captive aquatic animal husbandry. In most cases, you will need to select a school that offers you a good background in biology and then teach yourself the necessary husbandry topics. Some schools that do offer aquarium classes include Bowling Green State University in Ohio and the Oregon Coast Community College. Some enterprising young aquarists major in biology and minor in business. This gives them the knowledge about animals as well as how to operate a business such as a pet store or public aquarium.

Advancing in the Hobby

Glossary

acclimation: The process of gradually adapting an animal to a new environment.

algae: A simple photosynthetic organism that grows in aquatic environments.

ammonia: A chemical compound containing nitrogen that is a primary waste product of fish. It becomes toxic if allowed to build up in aquarium water.

aquatic: Living in, or related to, water.

aquarist: A person who works with aquariums and the animals they house. Some people are aquarists as a hobby; others do this for a career.

aquarium: A container holding water and aquatic organisms.

biological filtration: The process by which bacteria use the toxic waste products of fish as their food and, by doing so, change them to less toxic chemicals.

biological control: The use of one animal to control the population of a pest species in an aquarium. For example, using snails to control unwanted algae growth.

biomass: The total amount of living things in a given area, such as the biomass in an aquarium.

brine shrimp: A small aquatic crustacean, *Artemia salina*, often used as food for aquarium animals.

carnivore: An organism whose diet consists solely of animal protein.

caudal fin: The tail fin of a fish.

crustacean: A type of arthropod (joint-legged animal) with a hard shell. Includes crabs, crayfish and barnacles.

daphnia: Also known as water fleas, these tiny crustaceans are a very important live or frozen food for many small fish.

dorsal fin: The top fin(s) on a fish. Some fish have spiny dorsal fins.

ecosystem: A grouping of all living things in a given area, along with the non-living physical factors that affect them.

environment: The physical location where organisms live. This can be either their natural or captive environment.

filtration: The process by which waste products from organisms and particles in the water are collected and removed or detoxified.

fish: Includes the teleosts (bony fish), but elasmobranchs (sharks and rays) also belong to this group. There are more species of fish than any other type of vertebrate, with over 24,000 known types.

freshwater: A type of water that is low in salt content, as found in most rivers and lakes.

fungus: A simple organism that grows by consuming organic material. Growth is plant-like but fungi do not perform photosynthesis.

gonopodium: The reproductive organ of certain livebearing fishes such as guppies.

herbivore: An animal that derives its food energy from feeding on plant material.

infusoria: Also called green water, this is a culture of microorganisms used to feed baby fish.

invertebrate: Any animal without a spinal column such as a sea anemone, starfish, or snail.

krill: A small oceanic crustacean commonly used as a food for aquarium fish.

lateral line: A sense organ used by fish to detect vibrations in the water. The lateral line is usually visible as a faint line running lengthwise down each side of a fish, from the gill covers to the base of the caudal fin.

marine: Salt water, ocean water, as opposed to fresh water. There is also brackish water that is midway between these two types of water in terms of salt content.

mini-aquarium: A small aquarium that typically contains less than 8 gallons (30 liters) of water.

mini-reef: A marine aquarium of any size that houses live rock, corals, and usually contains an assortment of fish and invertebrates.

nitrate: A waste product formed by the process of biological filtration. It is measured as the concentration of nitrogen that is in the form of the nitrate ion.

nitrite: An intermediate compound formed during the process of biological filtration.

omnivore: An animal that feeds on both plant and animal material.

organism: Any living thing. In aquariums, this can be an animal, plant, bacteria, protozoan, or algae.

parasite: An organism that gains food energy from another living organism.

pectoral fins: The pair of clear, soft fins on either side of a fish, just behind its gills.

pelvic fins: A pair of fins located on the belly of a fish. A single anal fin is sometimes located behind the pelvic fins.

pH: The measure of acidity or alkalinity of a solution.

photoperiod: The length of time, usually measured in hours, that a photosynthetic organism is exposed to light each day.

photosynthetic: An organism that turns light energy, carbon dioxide, and water into simple sugars (chemical energy).

protozoan: A single-celled microorganism. Some protozoans are parasites of fish.

quarantine: A process by which potentially infective organisms are isolated from others to reduce the chance of spreading disease.

scientific name: Every living thing has a single scientific name. This is written in Latin and in the form of Genus species. For example, the scientific name for the guppy is *Poecilia reticulata*.

specimen: This term is used here to describe any plant or animal that is a primary resident of an aquarium.

substrate: Usually gravel or sand. Serves to cover the bottom of an aquarium.

tank: A less formal term for an aquarium.

temperate: Refers to an environment that is neither tropical nor arctic. In aquarium use, denotes a water temperature in the range of 45°F (7°C) to 74°F (23°C).

tropical: Used to refer to a warm environment with a narrow temperature range of around 75°F (24°C) to 85°F (29°C).

vertebrate: An animal with a backbone. Includes fish, amphibians, reptiles, birds, and mammals.

Resources

There are many resources you can use to increase your knowledge and enjoyment of your aquariums. One important source of information can be your local aquarium club. Larger cities have clubs whose members meet to learn more about aquariums, trade fish and equipment, and just to socialize with other people who share an interest in the hobby. Many clubs have yearly fish shows where people can compete with one another by displaying the best-quality fish or aquarium setup. Most clubs also have a newsletter to keep members informed about their activities. If you live in a town without an aquarium club, what about starting one yourself? For people without a local club, there are national organizations (some are listed below) that can fill many of the same roles as a local club does. Obviously, the Internet has truly changed how people interact, so now there are even many international aquarium organizations you can belong to. Some are even free to join.

The following lists include some of the best resources for intermediate-level aquarium hobbyists. Contact information can sometimes change and new books are written every year, but you can use this information as a starting point. Remember that your local pet store is also a great source for immediate information about your aquariums.

Aquarium Clubs

American Cichlid Association
Claudia Dickinson – Membership Coordinator
P.O. Box 5078
Montauk, NY 11954
631-668-5125
www.cichlid.org

American Killifish Association
Jim Randall
AKA Membership Committee
823 Park Avenue
Albany, NY 12208
www.aka.org

American Livebearer Association
Timothy J. Brady - Membership Chair
5 Zerbe Street, Cressona, PA 17929-1513
(570) 385-0573
www.livebearers.org

Canadian Association of Aquarium Clubs
David Boehm – Membership Chair
17 Hamel Avenue Kitchener, ON N2K 1M6 (519) 500-8419
www.caoac.ca/

Federation of American Aquarium Societies
Sam Borstein - Secretary
www.faas.info/index.html

International Fancy Guppy Association
Bill Carwile - Membership
921 Calohan Road
Rustburg, VA. 24588
434-821-3351
www.ifga.org

Books

Jay F. Hemdal *Advanced Marine Aquarium Techniques*

David E. Boruchowitz *Aquarium Care of Bettas*

Claudia Dickinson *Aquarium Care of Cichlids*

Neale Monks, Editor *Brackish Water Fishes*

Glen S. Axelrod, M.S., F.Z.S and Brian M. Scott *Encyclopedia of Exotic Tropical Fishes for Freshwater Aquariums*

David E. Boruchowitz *Freshwater Aquarium Problem Solver*

Martin A. Moe, Jr. *Marine Aquarium Handbook*

Terry Anne Barber *Setup and Care of Garden Ponds*

Internet Resources

Aquaria Central
http://www.aquariacentral.com/

Aquatic Community
http://www.aquaticcommunity.com/

FINS: The Fish Information Service
http://fins.actwin.com

FishBase – scientific information for all fish species
http://www.fishbase.org

Tropical Fishkeeping Forum
http://www.tropicalfishkeeping.com/

Magazines

Tropical Fish Hobbyist
1 TFH Plaza
3rd and Union Avenues
Neptune City, NJ 07753
(732) 988-8400
E-mail: info@tfh.com
www.tfhmagazine.com

Index

Index

Acknowledgements

I would like to extend my sincere appreciation to all the people who helped me with this effort: My wife and son, for their patience as I wrote in my home office, night after night. My employer, The Toledo Zoo, has always been extremely supportive of my writing efforts. The aquarium department staff there has always been eager to help with my projects and have offered many excellent suggestions over the years. Finally, I would like to thank my parents, John and Sally, who nurtured my early awareness of aquatic life despite their having absolutely no interest in the topic of aquariums themselves!

About the Author

Jay F. Hemdal has been an avid aquarist for over 45 years. He set up his first marine aquarium when he was 9 years old. He worked part time for many years at various local retail pet stores and fish wholesale companies while he was living at home and later at college. After graduating from college, he managed the aquarium department of a large retail pet store for five years until 1985, when he was hired as an aquarist/diver (and later department manager) for the John G. Shedd Aquarium in Chicago. In 1989, he accepted the position of curator of fishes and invertebrates for the Toledo Zoo, where he still works today. The aquarium at the Toledo Zoo exhibits over 3300 animals comprising over 325 different species including sharks, flashlight fish, giant spider crabs, giant octopus, exotic insects, as well as many other, more commonly seen species. Beginning in 2013, the Toledo Zoo Aquarium will be closed for a major two-year renovation and expansion. Jay has written over 150 magazine articles and five previous books since 1981. He lives with his wife Tammy and their son John Thomas in their home on the bank of the tranquil Raisin River, where they enjoy fishing, archery, and kayaking.

Photo Credits

Adisa (Shutterstock): 14
Radek Bednarczuk: 11
Elena Blokhina (Shutterstock): 66
Dr. Warren Burgess: 88
Parpalea Catalin (Shutterstock): 8
Albert Connelly, Jr.: 77
Richard Davis: 12 (bottom)
Mo Devlin: 82
Dobermaraner (Shutterstock): 52
Vasyl Dudenko (Shutterstock): 29
Colin Dunlop: 97 (top)
Ross Maria Fluza Sciullo Faria (Shutterstock): 10
Greg Gilmour: 101
Heidi Hart (Shutterstock): 4
Jay Hemdal: 59, 60
David Herlong: 31
Matt Jones (Shutterstock): 35
Igor Kovalchuk (Shutterstock): 12 (top)
Blaz Kure (Shutterstock): 62
Gary Lange: 48
Lim Tiaw Leong (Shutterstock): 71
Oliver Lucanus: 90
Leighton Lum: 42
William Attard McCarthy (Shutterstock): 36, 54

Laura Muha: 75
Tsing Mui: 8
Namsilat (Shutterstock): 67
Alias Studiot Oy (Shutterstock): 28
M.P. & C. Piednoir: 16, 49, 100
Zach Piso: 103
Chawalit S. (Shutterstock): 58
G. Schmelzer: 73
Craig Sernotti: 34, 80
Mark Smith: 20, 33, 86
Boris Sosnovyy (Shutterstock): 64
Iggy Tavares: 15, 87, 94
Tony Terceira: 17, 24, 43, 45, 56
Abramov Timur (Shutterstock): 7
Nikita Tiunov (Shutterstock): 50
Alexey U (Shutterstock): 40
M. Walls: 97 (bottom)
David Watson: 68
Joshua Wiegert: 89
Ed Wong: 13, 93
Andrzej Zabawski: 47, 98

All other photos courtesy of TFH Photo Archives.